CHRIS

ALPHA FORCE

RYAN

UNTOUCHABLE

RED
FOX

ALPHA FORCE: UNTOUCHABLE
A RED FOX BOOK : 978 0 099 48233 8

First published in Great Britain by Red Fox,
an imprint of Random House Children's Books

This edition published 2005

9 10 8

Copyright © Chris Ryan, 2005

The right of Chris Ryan to be identified as the author of this work has been
asserted in accordance with the Copyright, Designs and Patents Act 1988.

The Random House Group Limited supports The Forest Stewardship
Council (FSC), the leading international forest certification organisation.
All our titles that are printed on Greenpeace approved FSC certified paper
carry the FSC logo. Our paper procurement policy can be found at:
www.rbooks.co.uk/environment.

Typeset in Sabon by Palimpsest Book Production Limited,
Polmont, Stirlingshire

Red Fox Books are published by Random House Children's Books,
61–63 Uxbridge Road, London W5 5SA,
A Random House Group Company

Addr...   ...ted

A CIP ...   ...brary.

ALPHA FORCE

The field of operation...

SCOTTISH
HIGHLANDS

UNITED
KINGDOM

EUROPE

Prologue

THE ASTRONOMER

On a cold night in early spring James Fletcher climbed out of his hired Land Rover, checked the battery icon on his digital camera, ran his torch once more over his Ordnance Survey map and set off over the dark hillside.

He picked his way carefully over the boulders, using a ski pole to keep his balance. It was a clear night, the stars twinkling in tiny points. He identified Jupiter to the south, Saturn to the west, the full moon setting. He also identified the circumpolar constellations, Leo and Virgo on the ecliptic, Bootes with its bright star Arcturus, Coma Berenices and Hercules with the M13 globular cluster. James Fletcher's knowledge of the night sky was much wider than average – he was a professor of astronomy. He'd come to a holiday cottage far up in the north of Scotland to spend his Easter break photographing one of the night sky's most spectacular phenomena – the Northern Lights, or aurora borealis.

He'd seen them many times before but never failed to delight in them. Streams of ghostly greenish-blue light caused by electrically charged particles streaming off the sun and colliding with gases in the Earth's ionosphere. And just now there was plenty of solar activity, so tonight's display should be a good one. He was hoping to get some really special shots for his website.

He became aware of a sound – a vehicle was approaching. A white glow appeared from under the ridge: headlights coming up the steep slope. He smiled. Another astronomy nut, no doubt. Well, that was nice – he'd have company.

The headlights bounced up over the ridge. They

were closer together than a car's – probably one of those chunky quad bikes he had seen people travelling around on.

It *was* a quad bike. Over the noise of the engine he heard shouts. Two riders.

James waved. He thought they'd cut the engine and come and talk to him. They didn't. The headlights remained on, the engine idling. He couldn't see the riders because they were in shadow. But he heard them talking. One of them said, 'He's got a camera.'

It seemed a little unfriendly, but James was used to dealing with quirky scientists. Many of his colleagues behaved oddly when confronted with strangers. James held out his hand and walked over to introduce himself.

One of the riders shone a torch straight at him. It fixed on his eyes, flicked down his waterproof jacket and trousers to his boots, then went back up to his face. James put his hand up to shield his eyes and blinked through his fingers. 'Er – do you mind, you're dazzling me.'

A voice came out of the shadows. 'He's on his own.'

Something was wrong. They thought he shouldn't be there. 'Er, I'm sorry,' said James. 'I didn't think this was private property.'

'He's got a camera,' another voice repeated.

James heard someone step off the bike and approach him. But he couldn't see him, so he never saw the gun.

His last moments were a deafening noise, a blow like a sledgehammer – and a torch still shining in his eyes.

The man walked up close to the body and looked down at him. A sawn-off shotgun smoked in the crook of his arm. Birds and night animals screeched and hooted as the echo of the shot died down, but it wasn't an unusual thing to hear in these hills. He broke the breech of the shotgun and flicked the spent cartridge onto the grass. That wasn't an unusual thing to find in these parts either. A smell of cordite and gunpowder rose into the air, mingling with the smell of charred flesh.

'Is he dead?' asked his companion, still on the bike.

The man ran his torch over the body. James

Fletcher's throat and chin were a hole filling with dark blood.

The man on the quad lit a cigarette. 'Get that camera.'

The gunman peered closer at James Fletcher's ruined chest. Little pieces of glass and twisted metal twinkled in the dark, wet mess of flesh. The camera was smashed. 'It's not going to tell any tales,' said the man. 'What are we going to do with him?'

'Put him where we always put things we don't want to be found.'

1

INSTRUCTORS

'Listen up, guys.' Amber clapped her hands to get her audience's attention. 'As if you haven't put up with enough humiliation from us, here's one last ordeal. Come and get your certificate, Joe.'

It was a cosy, stone-built club room, with low beams and a big fireplace. The last rays of an August sun were setting outside, and inside the atmosphere was cheerful. Six teenagers were on the last night of an adventure holiday in the north of Scotland with Alex, Li, Paulo, Hex and Amber. Watching the whole proceedings was Mary, the youth co-ordinator.

Although she was in overall charge of the project, she was taking a back seat. This evening belonged to Alpha Force.

Right now, black American Amber was hosting the passing-out ceremony, her Boston accent and easy confidence making her a natural compere. When she called his name, Joe, a lanky, dark-haired fifteen-year-old, put down his pint of Coke next to his chair, pulled his hoodie over his face and stood up to collect his certificate. Wolf-whistles and a smattering of applause accompanied him back to his seat by the stone fireplace, where he sprawled gratefully and picked up his drink again.

'Joe also wins the Oscar for the most spectacular horse-riding stunt,' smiled Amber.

Her comment produced another barrage of cheers from the small audience as they remembered all too well a calamity that had happened during the week's holiday, when the quiet cob Joe was riding was stung by a wasp.

Amber looked down at the next certificate in her hands. 'Alice?'

There was more applause and a girl stepped

forward, her blonde hair held down by a red baseball cap.

'Alice deserves a Grammy for teaching Alex some new marching songs,' said Amber. 'Honestly, we can't thank you enough.'

Alex, in the corner, chuckled along with the rest. Their six charges looked happy enough now, but the adventure holiday had not started so well. None of them had wanted to be there. They'd been sent by their parents, who were desperate to wean them off PCs, X-boxes, PlayStations and iPods. The hostel, where the main activities on offer were abseiling, orienteering and kayaking, had come as a big shock. The kids were appalled.

They weren't the only ones. On that first night Alex, Hex, Li, Paulo and Amber wished they'd never agreed to take the project on. Their brief had been to introduce a group of city-bred teens to the joys of the wilds. But they had to force these kids to even go for a walk, let alone climb a mountain. Instead of sharing their love of the outdoors they were running a boot camp. When Alex drove them back to the hostel in the Range Rover at the end of the first day the rear-view mirror showed a row of hostile stares, white iPod wires framing their faces like stethoscopes. But bit by bit, something had changed. They began to enjoy the way a compass could make sense of a featureless wilderness of rocks and heather; the way you could kayak along the surface of a loch as silently as a fish; the way a couple of ropes and an abseil harness let you defy gravity. They stopped listening to their iPods on the journey back; they talked to each other about what they'd done that day.

In some ways, Alex thought, the week had been like a trip back in time. Back to when Alpha Force had first met, on a holiday crewing a sailing ship around the islands of Indonesia. Alex had loved it. The sea was like the open moors in Northumbria where he had grown up, only better. However, the other four people on his watch were not impressed. There was Hex from London, whose parents had sent him after he'd wreaked havoc hacking into a computer. There was Li, a striking, fine-boned Anglo-Chinese girl who skived off work by trapezing through the rigging. There was laid-back Paulo from a ranch in Argentina, who seemed to be on permanent siesta and could only be roused in order to flirt with Li. And there was spoiled American heiress Amber, who had recently lost her parents and hated the whole world. But after the group were marooned on a deserted island they became the closest of friends. When Amber found out that her dead parents had been human rights campaigners, this close-knit group of survivors wanted to carry on with their work. Now, every holiday they got together to hone their survival skills and hang out. And very often they found missions in the most unlikely places.

It was Amber's rich businessman uncle, John Middleton, who had found them this gig. A travel company owned by a friend of his had set it up and the original guides pulled out. He needed somebody to help run the adventure holiday at short notice. John Middleton knew the very people. And afterwards, the five friends would have a few days with the place to themselves.

Alex came back to the present.

'Fleur wins the Oscar for best director – for that lovely video of Paulo sliding into the loch on his ass.'

Another round of whistles, laughter and applause,

and a girl with long dark wavy hair made her way back to her seat, a certificate in her hands. Paulo's handsome face grinned under his curly mop. He gave Fleur a high five as she passed him to sit down.

The door opened. A petite blonde girl in cropped grey trousers came in and plonked herself down on the sofa next to Alice, her arms folded.

The group stared at her.

'Oh,' she said, noticing their attention. 'Did I just miss the group hug?' Her voice dripped with sarcasm. She stared at Amber and put her hand out. 'Come on, give it to me.'

Tiff's arrival had changed the easy-going mood of the room. Some of the kids looked down, not knowing what to do; others continued to stare at her.

Amber felt her hackles rise but tried to hide it. 'Give you what?'

Tiff popped a piece of gum into her mouth and looked at Amber as she started chewing. The way Tiff chewed was nothing like the way anyone else did. She chewed as if she was daring you to say something. She had chewed that way as she hauled her slight body up a mountain in deliberate slow motion; as she'd sat down during a hike and refused to walk another step. *Go on*, her chewing said. *What are you going to do about it?* The other kids had been just as difficult to start with, but as they started to enjoy themselves Tiff stayed mutinous. Now here she was at the bitter end, still rebelling.

The jaw chewed. 'Where's my crummy certificate?'

One of the things Alex was especially looking forward to was seeing the back of her. He answered her question. 'You don't get one. You haven't passed.'

Tiff turned her chewing face in his direction. 'They all got one.'

'They earned them,' said Li.

Tiff shrugged. She reached past Alice and grabbed the certificate on the arm of the sofa. Alice tried to grab it but Tiff held it out of her reach.

'Keep your hair on, I'm only looking.' Tiff studied the certificate for a moment, mouth working. Her face broke into a humourless grin. 'What a load of crap.'

'Just give it back,' said Alice.

Tiff held the certificate teasingly between pinched fingers, threatening to tear it in two. Now she really had everyone's attention. Slowly she ripped the certificate in two and let the pieces fall.

The entire room gasped.

Amber's eyes narrowed; Alex was looking at the girl with loathing; Hex's eyes were flinty; Li's knuckles were white as she gripped the chair, as though she was having trouble keeping herself from jumping up and giving the girl a good slap. Tiff sat back and glared at them all, arms folded, her mouth still chewing.

Paulo heard the chair scrape beside him. Mary slipped into the seat. 'Er, Paulo, can I have a word?'

Paulo grimaced. 'Pretty dumb show of authority, eh? Thank God we're getting shot of her.' He smiled at Mary, but Mary didn't respond.

'I have a problem. I had a fax from Tiff's parents. They've been delayed and asked if she could stay on for a bit longer.'

Paulo looked at the others. After the outrage, the cheerful mood was returning to the room. He knew without a doubt that the others were relaxing because they would soon be getting rid of Tiff. He said reluctantly, 'How long does she need to stay?'

'Until the weekend.'

The weekend. Today was Sunday. They'd have Tiff for another five days at least. That would be almost all of their time together. 'Are you staying too?' he said.

'I've got to leave tomorrow. Her parents are happy for you to be completely in charge, do what you want. I know she's a pain, but she hasn't got anywhere else to go.'

Paulo heard himself say, 'All right, we'll have her.'

But he dreaded what the others would say.

2

UNWANTED GUEST

Alex liked to sit outside last thing before going to bed. The sun had gone down, leaving a faint line of fire outlining the tops of the mountains. The white walls of the hostel were pinkish purple, the dark slate roof invisible against the black mountain. Lighted upstairs windows were squares of bright orange. Occasionally a shadow flitted across the curtains as the kids packed and got ready for bed. The hostel had started life as a couple of crofts nestled in the heather-covered hills. A two-storey house had been built to join them together, creating a sizeable building that could sleep twelve. They had rented it, through the holiday company, from the laird who owned Glaickvullin Lodge, further down the valley. All the land immediately around – a thousand hectares – belonged to his estate.

It was so peaceful. You only got that deep silence in a huge open space. It reminded Alex of his solitary camping trips on the Northumbrian moors, practising survival skills learned from his dad, a soldier in the SAS.

The north of Scotland was Alex's kind of place – the lochs that ran like silver tongues between the brooding mountains, the thrashing sea, the mists that rolled in like smoke, the heather-covered hills like rumples of purple tweed. He could imagine nothing nicer than cooking mussels and cockles over a pit of fire on a rugged seashore, watching the birds and seals with his four friends. There was Paulo, medic, engineering expert. His charm and easy laugh had meant that he was the first member of Alpha Force to win over the reluctant guests. There was Hex, their computer expert, virtually Paulo's opposite – a loner, preferring to observe or to retreat into the cyber-world of his palmtop computer. If Paulo had won the kids' affections, Hex had won their admiration with his knowledge of arcane websites. There was Li, martial arts expert, so petite that she looked fragile. But Alex had never met anyone with such strength. There was Amber, their navigation expert, who had chaired the evening's proceedings with relaxed assurance.

The thought came into Alex's mind, not for the first time: they were all getting older. They would be leaving school, making career choices. Amber's new responsibilities were just the beginning. Would this be the last holiday together?

Whether it was or not, he certainly didn't want it spoiled by an unwanted guest.

High up in a window in the central part of the building he saw a dim light and a familiar outline – Hex, his cropped head bent over his palmtop.

Alex grasped the drainpipe, tugged it to see if it would take his weight and climbed up swiftly, hand over hand. Hex was clicking on his palmtop keyboard with each ear enclosed by a silver cup. They were cordless Bluetooth headphones – his latest pride and joy.

That meant Hex wouldn't hear him coming. Alex smiled as he slipped in through the window.

Hex looked at him and gave a yelp, but a moment later Alex found himself slammed onto the window frame, his head dangling over the edge, the catch digging painfully into his back and a hand at his throat.

Alex kicked Hex's legs out from underneath him and he rolled away. Alex slid off the windowsill down to the floor and found Hex already crouching on his heels, ready to strike.

Alex relaxed and sat back against the wall, laughing. 'Sorry, mate, I couldn't resist it – your window was open.'

Hex relaxed out of the fighting posture. He retrieved his palmtop, which was upside down on the orange duvet, glowing blue like an upturned book of magic. He snapped it shut and sat on the bed.

Alex dusted flakes of black paint from the drainpipe off his hands. 'Great reaction time. Even with the headphones you didn't miss a beat.'

Hex pulled a face. 'If you'd been Paulo, I wouldn't

have stopped. He must be off his head. It was going to be just the five of us; now we have to haul that sourpuss around.'

Alex looked at him. 'Mate, take those off, you look like an alien.'

Hex remembered the headphones and unhooked them. 'What was Paulo thinking? Why on earth did he say yes?'

Amber had grabbed Paulo's phone and was not going to give it back. 'It's a message from Fleur.' She sat back on her bed, pulled her knees up to her chest and read out the text. '*Lovely to meet you. If you're ever in Manchester give me a call.*' Amber's eyes opened wide. 'Oooh, a fan.' She tossed the phone back onto the purple duvet.

Paulo watched from a chair, while Li sank back on her elbows at the foot of the bed. They were in Amber's bedroom, keeping out of the way of the kids, who were searching the common areas checking they hadn't left anything behind.

'I bet Fleur's hoping you'll ask her to stay another week too,' said Amber acidly.

'Bet she can't understand why you singled out a monster like Tiff to keep on,' said Li.

'Law of the jungle,' Amber told her. 'Nice girls finish last.'

Paulo grimaced. He normally gave as good as he got when they started teasing but right now he was thinking, What have I done?

Another bleep – another message. This time Li got to it first. Click, click-click. 'Claire.' She looked at Paulo. 'She says, are you free for a party in Ipswich next week?'

Paulo shook his head and winced again.

'We could all go to Ipswich, wherever that is,' said Amber. 'Instead, what have we got to look forward to?' Her voice took on a parodying whine. '*I can't do it . . .*'

Li joined in, matching Amber's tone perfectly. '*It's minging. This harness won't fit me, it's not small enough.*'

Amber reverted to her own voice. 'And the kayaks!' she exclaimed. 'She just sat in hers and drifted. She never even got her oars wet.'

'I think she just wanted Paulo to rescue her.'

'Well congratulations, Paulo – you can spend the next week rescuing her,' said Amber.

Another bleep. Li snatched Paulo's phone. 'Ooh. It's Tiff.'

Paulo sat bolt upright, glowering. 'It's not.'

Li tossed the phone to him. 'No. It's Alice.'

Paulo caught the phone and lay back in the chair, one hand over his heart as though calming it down. '*Dios*, you nearly killed me.'

Amber's phone bleeped on the bedside table. She had a text. 'Ah,' she said.

Paulo and Li looked at her. From the tone of the 'ah' the message was not good news.

Amber looked up. 'It's Mary. Tiff's parents are very grateful and have wired the necessary funds.'

3

THE CAVES

'Geronimo!' called Paulo. The tunnel was like a helter-skelter and he was sliding – fast. Millions of tiny fossils glinted in the light of his headlamp. It occurred to him that millions of them should also be grinding into his backside, too, only it felt nice and smooth. The tunnel must have been worn down by many sliding potholers.

He landed on his hands and knees in a cave. It smelled of wet rock and algae. He looked around. On the roof was what looked like an immense, wide chandelier – thousands of tiny stalactites, glittering in the light of his headlamp.

'Wow.'

They were exploring the potholes on the estate, etched out of the limestone over millions of years by natural water courses. Alex and Paulo had done a week-long course in caving leadership, and were now qualified to lead expeditions.

Alex's voice came down the tunnel. 'Paulo? Are you there?'

Paulo scrambled to his feet. 'Yeah, come on down.'

He heard a thudding and the sound of waterproof overalls slithering on rock. It grew louder and combined with a female voice whooping in excitement.

Amber was deposited at his feet. Like him, she looked around, saw the roof of stalactites and boggled. 'Awesome.'

Another body swished down the tunnel. Li slithered out and, unlike the others, landed on her feet.

'Were you cheating?' said Paulo. 'That was twice as fast as Amber.'

'I greased my overalls,' replied Li. Then she too noticed the ceiling. 'Wow.'

Another person was in the tunnel. Amber listened. 'I bet that's Hex.'

'How can you tell?' said Paulo.

'He doesn't sound like he's enjoying it. He's very quiet.'

Hex kept his eyes firmly on the spot of light beyond his feet. He just wanted it to be over. It was the thought of all that rock around and above him. No matter that it had been that way for centuries; today might be the day it moved – and then he would be crushed like one of those millions of insects that eventually became oil reserves. Whenever he'd been in confined spaces he'd had horrible experiences. And these potholes weren't like he'd imagined caves. They weren't the neat corridors of rock you saw in films. It was more like somebody had thrown a pile of rocks into a jar and they were squeezing between the gaps. There was no order to it – a big space could dwindle to a tiny crevice. It was all so haphazard; how could it be stable?

When he popped out, he breathed out with relief. But the relief was short lived. He was still in a cave, and the floor sloped sharply. Why couldn't anything be a simple, regular shape down here?

A sound of cursing came from the tunnel. Hex jumped out of the way. 'That's got to be Tiff.'

Tiff was deposited in the cavern. For a moment she looked around in wonder. Then her mask of indifference came down. She resumed tumbling the piece of gum in her mouth.

Alex came down last and they set off for the next landmark.

Paulo led the way, map in one hand, his other arm out to steady himself on the wet rock wall. He was enjoying himself – this hidden labyrinth was like a set of puzzles. Yes, it was wet and it was cold, but they were wearing fleeces under the waterproof overalls. Anyway, that kind of thing rarely bothered him. He'd spent most of his life out on his parents' ranch and was practically immune to the weather.

Alex was enjoying it too. Caving brought new challenges. Navigation was important. As they picked their way along, Amber kept a close eye on the compass. A wrong turning could get them seriously lost.

'This place is minging,' said a bored voice. 'It's really cold.'

'Keep moving and you'll warm up,' said Li.

Tiff stopped immediately, planting her feet. 'My knees are hurting. It's these pads.' She pointed to the black rubber knee pads she wore over her boiler suit. Her face looked tiny under the purple plastic helmet.

Hex, in front, grimaced at Amber. Being in the cave was bad enough. Having Tiff go on about it was like Chinese water torture.

'Take the pads off, then,' Li said.

Tiff held one leg out to her. 'You'll have to help me.'

Li raised an eyebrow. 'I think you're old enough to undress yourself.'

Paulo, at the front, knelt down to peer into what looked like a jagged hole.

'More crawling?' said Hex. He tried to sound enthusiastic. If he showed the slightest weakness, that monster Tiff would pick up on it and make it ten times worse.

'This mud,' said Paulo, 'has probably been here since dinosaurs walked the earth.'

Hex appreciated Paulo's attempt to cheer him up but it was still another hole.

'We're not all as keen on mud as you, Paulo,' said Li.

Paulo got down on all fours.

A voice piped up from the back. 'Can't I go at the front? All I can see is everyone's boots.'

Paulo looked back. 'There is nothing to see until we get out the other end. Anyway, as the guide I have to go first.'

He didn't hear what Tiff said next because he was already on his hands and knees in the hole. He heard the others coming behind him, then Hex said, 'Paulo – stop.'

Paulo stopped.

'The others aren't following.' Hex turned to look round. His helmet scraped on the roof; his elbows rasped against the wall.

Tiff was standing at the tunnel entrance holding her rucksack and the knee pads. 'You see,' she complained, 'I just needed someone to help me.'

Amber muttered, 'She's trying to waste time. She knows she can't get out of it so she's just trying to hold us up as much as possible.' She sat back to wait.

Eventually Tiff got into the tunnel with Li and

Alex following. They had only gone on a few metres when a plaintive voice said, 'Stop, please stop.'

Paulo stopped. 'What's wrong?'

'I haven't got knee pads.'

'You wanted to take them off,' said Alex.

'You didn't tell me we'd be doing this. And I can't use those ones, they're too big. I need the same size as she's got.' She pointed to Li.

'Mine are exactly the same as yours,' said Li. 'You adjust them.'

'These don't adjust. You haven't given me the proper equipment.'

Amber could see Hex's face pinching into a strained expression. He really didn't appreciate having to hang around in this tunnel. 'Let's get going,' she called, 'or we'll all die of cold.'

It had the desired effect.

'Die of cold?' exclaimed Tiff.

Paulo crawled on. Amber shut her ears and followed. At least they were all moving.

'We can die of cold down here?' insisted Tiff.

'Yes,' said Li behind her. 'The first symptom is that you talk too much.'

'You guys are dangerous,' said Tiff. 'You give me bad equipment, then you take it away so I've got nothing. This is minging. We could all die down here and no one would know. They'd find our skeletons in five hundred years.'

'We won't die down here,' said Alex patiently. 'We told the local caving club we'd be coming down. They know to come and find us if we don't check in with them later.'

Paulo, at the front, had to flatten out and crawl on his stomach. The roof came down even lower. He stopped. 'This is too narrow. We'll have to go back. Backwards, guys.'

Alex, who'd brought up the rear, started to squirm backwards on his hands and knees. Li's boots came swiftly behind, almost dinning on his helmet.

Back in the stalactite cavern again, Paulo and Amber checked the map and looked for another way through.

Tiff sat on a rock and folded her arms. 'Why did we turn round?'

'It's really small,' said Paulo. 'I couldn't get my shoulders through.'

'I could,' said Tiff.

'I could too,' said Li. 'But Paulo and Alex are our guides and they can't. So we don't go.'

'We've come all this way and you're chickening out.'

Li refused to rise to the bait. 'I thought you didn't like it down here.'

Amber tried to concentrate on her compass, although she dearly wanted to give Tiff a piece of her mind. She took a few steps towards a dark corner, then turned back. 'The tunnel's here, guys. This way.'

Paulo picked his way in front of her and got down on his hands and knees.

Tiff watched Hex follow Amber into the tunnel. 'On my knees again?' she complained. 'I haven't got any—'

'Just shut up, Tiff,' snapped Paulo. 'Get in the tunnel.'

Tiff sat back on her heels, her face outraged under her too-big helmet. 'Man, you are well out of order. Did everyone hear that? I'm cold, my knees hurt, I'm doing my best and he abuses me.'

The others looked at her coldly.

Tiff got down and crawled into the tunnel.

For a while they continued in a silent line. Paulo, at the front, was mortified. Losing his temper was unprofessional; it was bad manners; it was childish . . .

The tunnel became higher. They got to their feet and started to walk normally, easing out stiffened limbs.

But not for long. Soon they came to a shallow lake and a sheer wall. A vertical crack led away, its floor flooded.

Alex peered in. 'How deep is that?' He threw a stone. It splashed and ripples spread out in circles. It was only about ten centimetres deep.

Paulo waded into the water. His body was silhouetted against the glow from his headlight as he bent down. 'Another small one, I'm afraid,' he said, splashing along the tunnel.

Amber braced herself. Surely Tiff would have an opinion on that. But she seemed to have gone as quiet as a mouse.

'Where's Tiff?' asked Alex.

Paulo stopped splashing. The others looked around. There were only four of them in the cavern.

Alex looked back into the gulley they'd just come down. 'Tiff?'

But Tiff had gone.

4

STALAGMITE CAVERN

Amber put her hand to her head and groaned. 'Oh no. This is just brilliant.'

'She was in front of me when we came out of the narrow bit,' said Li.

Paulo splashed impatiently back into the cavern. 'I bet if we go back the way we came we'll find she's having a sit down.' But he felt guilty. Maybe he'd really upset her. Although there had been no other tunnels off the one they had just come along, there were numerous nooks and crannies. He peered into every one. Some were just small cracks when you got up close; some were big enough to crawl into.

The others followed. 'What if she's hurt herself?' said Alex. 'We're responsible for her. How could we have not noticed her dropping behind?'

'I think we'd have heard the screams,' muttered Li.

They were irritated, but they had to consider other possibilities. Getting a casualty out would be extremely difficult. And if she'd done more than just sit down, or gone back further than the last cave, she could be lost. How long would it take to find her?

Paulo emerged first into the stalactite cavern. 'Tiff?' he called.

Amber came out next, then the other three.

They stood and listened for movement. The only thing they could hear was the steady drip of water.

Then a feeble voice: 'Help.'

It came from the tunnel they had abandoned.

The five friends exchanged weary glances. So she had decided to take the shortest route to the top and leave the rest of them behind. But she hadn't looked at the map: the tunnel wasn't just an easy stroll up to the ground, and now she was in trouble.

Paulo knelt down and shone his headlamp into the hole. He couldn't see anything, just the tunnel getting narrower and narrower. 'Tiff?' he called.

'I'm here.'

'Are you hurt?' he called.

'No. I can't get out.'

'Try coming backwards,' said Li.

'I have,' said Tiff. 'I'm stuck.'

Hex said in a low voice so that his voice wouldn't carry, 'Well, that serves you right, doesn't it?'

Amber nodded.

Li looked at Paulo. 'How narrow was it down there?'

'Just your size,' said Paulo.

Li gave him a long-suffering look. She took off her rucksack and handed it to him, checked the rope slung diagonally across her body, then got down on her hands and knees.

Without the rucksack she reached the narrow section in no time. She had to squirm along on her belly like a lizard. It was like climbing along the inside of a drainpipe. Her breathing echoed, emphasizing how tiny the space was. She'd never been claustrophobic before but this was really unpleasant. She felt very alone. She kept reminding herself that her friends were back at the other end, friends who knew what to do if she got into trouble. The tunnel began to slope up steeply. She scrabbled to find handholds to pull herself up.

The tunnel suddenly turned downwards like an elbow. Li had visions of getting stuck round the corner. But Tiff had got through, so she could. In fact, thought Li as she squeezed around the gap, how did that little minx manage to get all this way? She must be tougher than she looks.

Li could see a ghostly white glow below her. A lamp. 'Tiff – are you there?' she called.

'Yes.' Tiff's voice sounded shrill. Was she frightened? Good, thought Li. She deserves to be. Next time she won't go off on her own.

Li's headlamp illuminated a patch of brown mud as she inched her way down the steep tunnel. The floor was only a metre further down now. She vaulted lightly into the cave.

Tiff was sitting on the floor, her helmet off, looking miserable, but not injured – it was her usual sulky expression. As Li looked around she saw a forest of big, jagged stalagmites, sticking up from the uneven floor like teeth in a shark's mouth.

For a moment she forgot that she was mad with Tiff. 'Wow,' she said. 'You've found a pretty amazing place.'

'Yeah, well, I want to go back now,' said Tiff curtly. She got up.

Li turned back to the tunnel to see how easy it was going to be to climb out. 'Did you try to get out?'

'Yeah. It's impossible.'

Li looked at her balefully. 'Well, I very much hope it isn't, or we're both stuck.'

Tiff jigged nervously from foot to foot. 'Come on, man, this is horrible in here. There's this noise.'

'That's not unusual in potholes,' said Li. 'It's probably underground water.' She inspected the tunnel. The first part was a slippery slope – there were scuff marks where Tiff had tried to climb back up. Li was an experienced climber and could see tiny handholds but for Tiff it would be impossible.

A squeal interrupted Li's thoughts. She turned round sharply. 'What?'

Tiff's eyes were blazing. 'Did you hear it?'

And then Li made out a sort of chugging, booming noise. It wasn't water. It was regular, with a beat. In the toothy gloom of the cave, it was rather eerie. It surged, as though giving more power, then settled to a steady chug again. Like an engine.

'See?' Tiff was angry. 'You thought I was making it up. You people never listen.'

'I'm sure there's a perfectly normal explanation,' said Li. 'Or are you still frightened of monsters under the bed?'

Tiff looked at her with contempt. 'You should learn some manners. Remember I'm the customer.'

Li bit her tongue. 'I sense you have hostility issues,' she said. 'Maybe we should have a group hug.' Actually she would never do anything of the sort, but it was worth it for the look of revulsion on Tiff's face.

Li hopped up into the tunnel mouth. 'You stay here and I'll go up and throw you this rope.'

'You won't be able to climb out,' said Tiff scornfully. 'I kept slipping.'

But Li was already scaling the steep slope, feeling

for tiny ledges with her fingers and toes. Slowly she made her way up to the elbow, then turned and threw down the rope for Tiff.

The sun was going down, splashing the sky with oranges, pinks and purples. Paulo and Hex were sitting on the terrace at the back of the hostel, watching an enormous display projected onto the white wall at the end of the building. On the display, three dots were moving around on a map like characters in a computer game. The dots were tracking devices – which the group used on missions. Hex and Paulo had found some projection equipment in the hostel and improvised a way to enlarge the palmtop display to the size of a cinema picture. With the help of some up-to-the-minute phone technology they had reinvented hide and seek – Alpha Force style.

Somewhere in the hostel, Alex was hiding. The others were split into teams, communicating via phones and hands-free cordless Bluetooth earpieces. Paulo was guiding Li in the house and Hex was guiding Amber. The winner was the first team to find Alex and take him prisoner. And it was getting very heated.

The boys spoke in low voices, their deckchairs just far enough apart that they couldn't hear each other. The projector was in between them, its whirring competing with the evening noises of crickets.

'Left, Li,' muttered Paulo, his eyes fixed on the screen. The hands-free headset was a small curl of silver plastic that hooked over his ear and rested on his cheekbone.

'Upstairs, first room on the left,' whispered Hex to Amber. On the screen he could see Amber was getting close to Alex, but Li was too. 'Hurry,' he urged. 'Li's in the next room.'

Alex's dot moved. He was getting away! Suddenly all the dots converged. From an open window on the landing came the sound of shrieks. The girls were giving chase.

It was too late for subtlety now. Paulo stood up and shouted encouragement at the screen. 'Go on, Li!'

Inside, Li saw Alex sprint for the stairs. Right, she'd head him off. The stairs went round and round, forming a square well. She vaulted over the banisters and dived for the lower handrail, catching it and vaulting over like a trapeze artist. In moments she was standing on the bottom stair looking up at Alex, the headset still in place, her phone in a zip pouch at her belt.

Alex's expression went through several very entertaining phases. First there was triumph as he pounded down the stairs, his feet a blur like a tap dancer. Then there was disbelief as he saw Li in front of him; then horror as he saw he was going to run smack into her.

Moments later he was tumbling over her back. She had ducked and rolled him over her. He curled himself into a ball to cushion his landing. Li put her foot on his chest, as though he was a lion she'd bagged.

Paulo raced in through the front door as Amber slid down the banister. 'Foul,' she called. 'Contestants aren't allowed to fly.'

'There are no rules about that,' panted Li. She took her foot off Alex. He sat up, rubbing his elbow.

Hex came in holding the palmtop, which he'd disconnected from the projector. 'That was just the beta test to iron out bugs. It doesn't count.'

'Rubbish,' said Paulo. 'We were victorious.'

Alex got to his feet. 'Let's see if Tiff wants to play.'

'She won't,' said Hex. 'She's watching a week's worth of *EastEnders* on video.'

Alex got to his feet. 'It won't do any harm to ask.'

He made his way down the hall to the TV room and knocked, but there was no answer. Perhaps Tiff couldn't hear him: the sound was turned up very high. He opened the door and peeked in.

He looked back at the others. 'She's not there. And the window's open. She's left the TV on and scarpered.'

'Hex?' called Amber. 'Need some magic here.'

Hex went into a small room off the main corridor. It was the hostel office. A filing cabinet was open and Amber sat at a desk looking at the addresses of all the kids who had been on the course the previous week, including their mobile numbers.

'I just called Tiff's mobile and she's engaged. See if you can trace her.' She pulled the Bluetooth headset out from behind her ear and put it on the desk.

Hex got out his palmtop. 'No problem.' Amber pushed her phone across the desk. Hex read the number off the display and typed it in. 'Just finding her network now . . . Keep phoning her in case she ends her call.'

Hex could only trace her as long as she was using the phone. It was illegal, of course, and well beyond most hackers, but Hex was in a league of his own. There wasn't a firewall he couldn't slip past, a password he couldn't crack. Now he was in the computer belonging to her phone company. Mobile phones were a good way to track somebody because they only worked if they were near a transmitter, or cell. Hex just had to find out which cell was taking her signals at the moment. It wasn't as accurate as the tracers Alpha Force wore, but it would narrow her position down to within a hundred metres or so.

Amber put her phone on the desk. 'The signal's gone. She's switched it off or gone out of range.'

Paulo and Alex came in with the projection equipment and laid it carefully on the floor.

'Doesn't matter,' said Hex. 'I've got her.' He turned his palmtop round. 'Find that grid reference.'

Li plucked an Ordnance Survey map from the bookshelf. She spread it out and located the co-ordinates. 'Hex, are you sure?'

Hex glanced at her impatiently. 'Transmitters don't lie.'

She looked up at the others. 'It's a disused railway tunnel.'

Amber frowned. 'What on earth's she doing there?'

Alex got down to practicalities. 'Do we take the Range Rover or the quad bikes?'

Paulo looked a bit sheepish.

Li glared at him accusingly. 'You're not still tinkering with the Range Rover?!'

Paulo looked pained. 'There's something a bit dodgy with the ignition system. You know I like to have things perfect.'

'Quads it is,' said Alex.

5

THE RAILWAY TUNNEL

Three quad bikes spun gravel. Then the fat tyres bit, and they zoomed off the drive and bounced up into the moorland.

Hex, in the lead, pushed the bike up to top speed, keeping a careful eye on the ground. Amber, on the seat behind him, was in charge of the palmtop, navigating as straight a route as possible to the tunnel. As well as being a powerful computer the tiny machine was a global positioning system or GPS, using military satellites to pinpoint their position anywhere in the world. Paulo and Li followed on another bike and Alex was on the third.

But a 'straight' route didn't mean straightforward. The riders constantly swerved around clumps of heather, rocks and gullies. At a top speed of fifty-six kph, if the quads hit an obstacle they would turn over.

Amber nudged Hex in the ribs and he adjusted the bike's course. Beyond the pool of light given out by his headlamps the night was pitch black. A railway tunnel, Amber thought. What was Tiff doing there? She must have gone to meet someone. What kind of trouble could she be getting into?

A glow of light was growing in the distance. At first she thought it was reflected headlights from a road: surely they'd vanish again. But they didn't. The area of light became bigger. She looked at the palmtop. 'That's it,' she hissed in Hex's ear.

Hex slowed. The others braked. There was a cluster of arc lights, and figures moving around. Something was going on there.

Paulo stopped. 'Let's leave the bikes and go in on foot.'

They cut their engines. They expected silence but instead there was a noise. A rhythmic thumping.

A vehicle pulled up under the arc lights. A couple of figures got out and then it drove off. A door opened and a red light appeared briefly. The sound changed, as if the treble had suddenly been turned up on a hi-fi. Music: fast, tinkly synths. The door closed again and it had gone.

'It's a rave,' said Hex.

Paulo groaned. 'Don't say we've got to haul her out. I'm too young to be a party pooper.'

'Let's look at this logically,' said Amber. 'She's fourteen. What would her parents say if they knew she was going to a rave?'

Alex took out a small torch and they began to walk towards the entrance.

'You know those horrible prefects who are always spoiling your fun, telling you off for running in corridors?' said Li. 'I feel like that.'

'We've got to get her out,' said Alex. 'She's not even old enough to go into pubs and buy drinks. We're supposed to be looking after her.' He grimaced. 'I sound so square.'

At the entrance was a circle of people waiting to pay. Their faces were painted with glitter and they wore strings of fluorescent beads around their necks and backpacks with cartoon characters. One by one they put their hands to their mouths and swallowed, then passed around a bottle of water. Amber caught a glimpse of lips closing around a white pill.

She leaned across to the others. 'There are drugs here – we've got to get her out.'

Hex looked at her. 'Stop jigging like that.'

Amber hadn't realized she was moving in time to the music. She nudged him. 'Go on, loosen up a bit.' He glared at her.

The group in front of them was now being searched by a pair of burly figures in black. Li looked down at her cut-off jeans and hiking boots. 'I think we're a bit underdressed. Do you think they'll let us in?'

Alex felt the urge to laugh. After all the dangerous things he'd done this was the first time he'd been searched for a weapon – on the way into a party. He was glad he'd left his knife at the hostel.

The music was crashingly loud, like overhead thunder. A strobe light threw blue-white flashes around the cavernous room. The air smelled of sweat and warm bodies. The ravers carried glow sticks – fluorescent tubes – swinging them in patterns as they danced.

Paulo stopped and stared. The last time he'd seen so many glow sticks was when they had been trapped by an earthquake in Belize – during a night of dust, rubble and death. Seeing a mass of writhing bodies drawing circles with them in a darkened railway tunnel was like an eerie flashback. He looked at Li and caught her eye.

She mouthed at him. '*Déjà vu.*'

He nodded.

It was impossible to talk. Alex turned to the others and they used hand signals. They'd split up and search the room.

Hex and Amber made for the crowd of gyrating bodies. Amber was definitely grooving, an enormous smile on her face. Any moment, thought Hex, she would explode like a dervish and be lost in the mass of bodies. He followed, and before he knew it he was taking steps in the same rhythm. Everywhere were these glow sticks, like radioactive bars of candy. He looked at the girls carefully, at the swinging ponytails, the glittery faces.

Alex picked his way to a quieter area, where people sat cross-legged on the floor, drinking water, sucking lollipops. He saw a petite figure sitting with her back towards him and touched her on the shoulder. She turned round and offered him a bracelet made of Dolly Mixtures. It wasn't Tiff. Alex shook his head and moved on.

At the other end of the room he ran into Li. She looked back and pointed at Paulo, who was moving with a kind of speeded-up salsa step around a group of girls.

Li had attracted some attention. A guy in baggy jeans with a chain hanging out of his pocket was offering her a bottle of water and putting his arm around her. She was clearly rejecting him but the guy persisted. If he went much further, thought Alex, Li might have to do something rather unfriendly.

Alex went up to her and grabbed the bottle. Li put her arm around him and gave his waist a squeeze. Alex nodded at the guy and took a swig of water.

The guy looked annoyed. Still, he got the message and went away.

Li mouthed a word at Alex. 'Tiff?'

Alex shook his head.

A wave of artificial smoke began to creep through the crowd, lit up in spots by the glow sticks and strobes. That would make it even more difficult to see who was there. Paulo emerged from the glowing fog like an apparition. He was closely followed by an emphatically grooving Amber and a jigging Hex.

Alex looked at them enquiringly. They shook their heads. He gave another hand signal: go round again; split up.

Again they disappeared into the flashing fog. Through the throng of bodies, in a strict search pattern, pushing past girls wearing butterfly wings, inspecting their glittery faces.

So many people; how long would they have to search?

Alex suddenly felt as if he'd closed his eyes for a minute and been rebooted, like a computer. What was he doing? He looked at the people dancing around him, their eyes half-closed. He'd spoken to that girl with the pigtails, the girl next to her with the glasses . . . Had he been there for days? No, it felt like he'd just arrived.

It was all familiar, but nothing was the same. With all these glow sticks it was like being back in Belize. All these bodies . . . but here there were far more of them. The faces around him turned into a group of schoolchildren and teachers, the people they'd been trapped with during the earthquake. Some of them were dead before he even found them; some of them died before he could get them out. Hex had been lost for hours that night. The relentless pulse of the music became like a sinister countdown. And yet all these people were staying here, dancing, the strobe picking out one after another like a hand of fate. *Get out*, he wanted to scream to them. *It's not safe. You're all going to die.*

Alex leaned against the rough brick walls and breathed deeply. What was happening to him?

Hex came towards him, a pink glow stick in his hand. It was so good to see him alive. Alex wanted to hug him, but then Paulo appeared – with Tiff. She was trudging along as usual, a white circular glow stick pulled down over her head like a fallen halo.

Get a grip, Alex told himself. *Get some air*. Gratefully, he led the way to the exit. As the door closed and cut off the music the cold air hit him like a shower and he saw that the others were out there too.

'Are you OK, Alex?' asked Li. 'You look a bit weird.'

Alex nodded. 'It was hot in there. I'm fine.'

Tiff was sticking next to Paulo, her mouth chewing. Aside from that her expression was blank, as though she was trying to mentally withdraw. With the glitter on her face and the pink streaks in her hair, she looked like a mannequin. Paulo looked closely at her – did she seem normal? Had she taken something? She stared back at him. He decided she was just her usual sulky self. He had been intending to give her a piece of his mind but if he said anything he'd just get that stony stare. At least she was coming without an argument.

At last the hostel was quiet. Tiff had gone to her room in silence. That was the only time she made any kind of noise – when she slammed the door. She refused to answer their questions about where she had found out about the rave.

The others went to bed but Alex's nerves were like live wires. He got dressed and went outside, but instead of absorbing the stillness of the moors, he couldn't keep still.

He patted his belt for his survival tin, which he carried everywhere. It contained an assortment of useful kit such as dry kindling and waterproof matches. What he was looking for was the tiny torch and the button compass. He replaced the lid and fastened it with waterproof tape. In his other pocket was his mobile. Now he could get moving.

He jogged down the drive and onto the moors. He could hear so many sounds: the wind blowing in the heather like a mini-gale; a lone car in the distance, its engine impossibly loud; the piercing cries of owls out hunting. His breathing deepened into his running rhythm and he felt better. Underfoot he felt rocks and springy turf and rocks. He ran, on and on.

A freak gust of wind brought a sound to him like the deep booming bass of the music in the rave. With it came images of smoke and glow sticks. The smoke turned into falling rubble, then rock dust, the glow sticks scattered like broken toys. The faces became still and stared at him, their dead eyes saying, *Why did I die?*

Alex slowed to a walk. He put his hands over his eyes, but the images were inside his head; they wouldn't go away. 'We couldn't save you all,' he whispered. 'We did all we could.'

Ahead of him was a lighted window. He had come to a building. It was golden and welcoming, a normal-looking thing. Maybe the light would chase these demons away. He stumbled towards it and peered in.

Two men were inside. Their mouths and noses were covered by green surgical masks. Their hands were bleached to corpse paleness by rubber gloves. One of the masks was moving, talking quietly to the other. There was blood spattered on them, and on the gloves. It was like the masks had taken over their faces, dissolved their lips. The other mask talked. It sounded like a low rumble, like gurgling blood. When the man took the mask off his mouth would be a bloodied hole.

Alex gasped and flattened himself against the wall, looking out into the night, breathing hard. By his feet, in the pool of light from the window, was something dark and quivering. He looked at it. Grey-pink snakes glistened in the shadows. They slithered in a heap, tying themselves in endless knots. Suddenly they made a high, piercing noise like a squeal of feedback. Beside them, a heart the size of a baby's fist beat on the rocky ground with a deep, heavy throb. As the snakes writhed and squealed Alex saw other fleshy items – the missing lips of the men inside. He glimpsed something round with an edging of white. It was worse than he thought. The men's eyes were starting to dissolve too and were being discarded out here.

Once the men had been absorbed, the masks might come and get him too. Alex stumbled away.

6

LONG NIGHT

Hex closed the bathroom door and went back to his bedroom. That's funny, he thought. I didn't leave the light on.

Suddenly he was ambushed. He caught a glimpse of Alex's blond hair, then he was engulfed in strong arms. Hex prepared to break free – until he realized this wasn't a judo hold. It was a hug.

'Mate,' said Alex, 'it is so good to see you alive.'

Hex froze. Something was really, really wrong. Alex wasn't the touchy-feely type. That sort of thing made Hex cringe too. It was why he liked computers so much. They did what you asked; no complicated stuff.

He disengaged himself from Alex's hug and held him at arm's length. 'Alex, what's happened?'

His friend's expression didn't look normal.

'Alex,' said Hex firmly, 'look at me.'

'You're alive,' said Alex, and made to hug him again.

Hex dodged and looked at Alex's eyes. The pupils were wide black holes and the eyes were flickering from side to side. He was grinding his teeth together.

'Alex, did you take anything at the rave?'

Something seemed to click in Alex's brain. For a moment he looked lucid. 'I am having,' he said, 'the most horrible trip.'

That cold sensation spread all over Hex's body again. They'd all been drinking water at the rave – had Alex's been spiked? And with what? It was the only explanation. Hex didn't know much about recreational drugs but he knew that they tended to enhance whatever was going on in your head. If you were worried, a drug would make you pathologically paranoid.

He steered Alex to the bed. 'Sit down. Stay there, I'm going to help you.'

Alex obeyed, like a child.

Hex knew he had to check first if Alex was in danger. He listened to his breathing. It was a bit fast, like someone who'd had a scare. It didn't look as though his airway was about to close.

Alex began muttering, 'I'm so sorry. It took us so long to find you.'

Hex sat back and looked at him. Alex didn't need a doctor – there probably wasn't an antidote anyway and a doctor would just tell them to keep an eye on him.

Alex hung his head. 'We looked for so long. So many dead people.'

Something was going on in Alex's head, thought Hex. What could he do about that? His palmtop was on the bedside table. That might do the trick. Hex put the cordless Bluetooth headphones over Alex's ears.

Alex looked at him. 'We didn't know where you were. The earthquake had brought down the room.'

Hex suddenly realized that Alex wasn't talking

paranoid gibberish; he was talking about the earthquake in Belize.

'Alex,' he said severely. 'Quiet. I'll have you sorted out in a moment.' The one thing Hex didn't want to do was to relive those memories.

The palmtop was on, the screen glowing. He brought up folders of music. Something nice to chill him out was what Alex needed. Most of Hex's collection was a bit dark; bound to make Alex worse. He clicked through the albums he had on MP3. Aim: *Cold Water Music* – definitely chilled, but a bit edgy, and track nine, 'Demonique', would scare the willies out of him. Autechre: *Amber* – no, too mysterious and a bit dark. He tended to listen to that when he was in a grim mood at school. *Buddha Bar 1* – a friend had sent it electronically by File Transfer Protocol and he hadn't got round to deleting it. But track one was celestial choirs, gentle percussion and harps. Definitely calming. He hit PLAY AND REPEAT. The familiar patterns of the first track leaked out of the headphones in a tinny voice.

Hex sat down cross-legged on the floor. Alex looked scared, like a rabbit caught in a car's headlights. Was the music too ethereal, too freaky? Hex couldn't think of anything else to try.

Then Alex began to look calmer. He lay down on Hex's bed.

The track reached the end and started again at the beginning. Hex stayed where he was, sitting on the floor, watching his friend.

When Alex woke up, his mouth was dry and his jaw ached. Someone was knocking at the door. He sat up. 'Yeah?' he said. He suddenly realized he wasn't in his own room.

Amber came in. 'Hex, it's our turn to do breakfast . . .' She trailed off as she saw Hex sitting with his back to the wardrobe. 'Unusual sleeping position.' Then she spotted Alex. 'Did I miss a slumber party?'

Alex realized he had something on his ears. Hex's Bluetooth headphones. He took them off and noticed that on the bedside table the lamp was on and Hex's palmtop was showing the 'battery dead' symbol. Then he remembered.

'Alex got drugged at the rave,' said Hex.

Amber's eyes went wide. 'You whaaat?'

He got to his feet. 'You sleep a bit longer if you need to, Alex. I'm going to get a shower.' He grabbed a towel from a chair.

Alex subsided back on the bed.

Li looked down at Paulo's legs poking out from under the Range Rover, and nudged him with her foot.

Paulo slid out from under the vehicle, then wished he hadn't. He wasn't on a small trolley, like the one he used at home to tinker with vehicles on the ranch. He was lying on the hard gravel drive. He'd have gravel rash for days.

Li was holding out a mug of coffee; Hex and Amber, behind her, were clutching theirs.

'Conference,' said Li. 'Before Tiff gets up. Did you feel OK after the rave?'

Paulo got to his feet, rubbing his sore back, and took the coffee. 'Huh?'

'Alex's water was spiked,' explained Hex. 'I found him having hallucinations. And flashbacks to Belize. Did you feel OK when we got back?'

Paulo nodded. 'Fine. Is Alex all right?'

'I think so. Just tired and bewildered now. I had a

quick surf around the web and it looks like one of these designer drugs – ecstasy mixed with something.'

'It was that guy.' Li's mind went back to the previous night in the rave. 'This guy was hitting on me, trying to get me to drink something. Alex drank it instead to scare him off.'

'What did he look like?' said Paulo. 'Maybe we can track him down.'

'He was a dork,' said Li. 'He was too sappy to be a drug dealer.'

'Anyway, he could have come from anywhere,' said Hex. 'I did some sleuthing last night and that rave had been advertised in a web community. Tiff probably knew about it for ages. No wonder she didn't complain when she had to stay.'

Paulo groaned. 'When's the next rave? Maybe she's doing the tour.'

'Not for a while,' said Hex. 'It's in Liverpool in October.'

They heard footsteps on the gravel. Alex was coming out of the kitchen, his hands curled around a mug of coffee. He looked pale, there were hollows under his eyes and he was moving gingerly.

'Hey,' he said, looking at the little group around the Range Rover. 'Is it working yet?'

'It'll go like a dream,' said Paulo. 'How do you feel?'

'So-so. Reckon I need to get out and do something. What's planned for today?'

'I was hoping we could do some climbing,' said Li, 'but that uses similar muscles to potholing and I don't think Tiff will cope. She'll be quite stiff after yesterday.'

'She wasn't stiff when I saw her dancing last night,' commented Paulo.

'No,' agreed Amber, 'but we should do something gentle or she'll refuse to do anything at all. How about orienteering? Alex, what do you feel like? You don't have to come with us.'

'Actually I could do with a run,' said Alex. 'To clear my head.'

'Someone should go with you,' said Paulo. 'You can get flashbacks with some drugs.'

'I'll go,' volunteered Hex. 'I'll bring the chill-out kit.'

They heard swearing and crashing from the kitchen. Tiff had come down.

'I think I hear her ladyship's up and about,' sighed Amber.

As they started back indoors, Alex hung back with Hex. 'Thanks for sorting me last night. I guess I was talking gibberish.'

'Snakes and Wendy houses,' said Hex. 'Yeah, you were.'

Alex kept his voice quiet. 'Can I ask a favour? Will you come with me to find that little house? I know it's daft but I want to see what's really there.'

7

FLASHBACK

Hex and Alex jogged across the open moor. Hex had an Ordnance Survey map in a waterproof case secured to his belt. Although Alex couldn't remember where he'd been, a little detective work allowed them to retrace his steps. While the palmtop finished recharging, they worked out how far he could have gone in the time, then looked on the map for possible buildings within that radius. It was mostly open moorland, and every farm, cottage or ruin was marked. It wasn't hard to narrow down Alex's likely route.

Hex kept looking at his friend as they jogged, worried he might get a relapse. But Alex seemed more normal now. He'd lost the washed-out pallor and the haunted eyes. In fact it was Hex who was looking worse. He'd only had about an hour of sleep because he'd been looking after Alex.

It was magnificent countryside. Rolling hills, narrow sheep tracks, hummocks where marshes had dried out, the occasional gulley carved by streams, now dried to just a trickle in the bottom. Some were more than a metre deep, covered with tufted wiry grass. But it wasn't quite as peaceful as during the night. Every now and again they heard the crack of a rifle shot in the distance – people from the hunting lodge. And sometimes—

A vast noise suddenly filled the sky. Hex and Alex stopped and looked up. A black shape like a dart zoomed over, heading out to sea. The RAF flew up from Lincolnshire to practise laser target marking on the uninhabited islands off the coast. The jet screamed into the distance, leaving a cotton-wool wake.

Hex's heart soared. Now he felt like he was in the land of the living again.

'Hey,' said Alex. He pointed ahead: on the horizon was a small stone building with a chimney and a fence.

Hex checked the map. It was marked, but there were no roads or tracks to it. He recognized the characteristic features. 'It's a bothy.'

They had come across a number of bothies in the previous week. They were small one-room buildings in the middle of nowhere, constructed so that travellers could shelter from bad weather. A club kept a number of them maintained as a tradition of the countryside.

But this one had fallen on hard times. As they approached, they saw that the fence petered out around the side of the building and became a mess of shattered wood. Where the rafters had been was open sky. The windows had gone and the interior was a mass of fallen timber.

Alex looked at it in disbelief. 'It was like this; it had a window here, but inside . . .'

'Maybe when the moonlight touched it, it came alive,' said Hex.

Alex gave him a withering look.

'Sorry, mate, but you were high as a kite and seeing snakes and faces. You might easily have imagined you saw people inside it.'

'No, there definitely were people,' insisted Alex. 'Let's have a look at the map.'

Hex handed it over.

Alex scanned the area around them, then compared it with the compass. 'There's another one just over that hill.' He set off at a jog.

Hex sighed. 'Just over the hill' was quite a way. Still, he liked to do at least one really long run every week.

They jogged up to the next peak. Down below was another small bothy with grey slate tiles. 'That's it,' panted Alex. 'It's got a roof.'

Don't get your hopes up, thought Hex as he followed him down.

This bothy was in much better condition. There was glass in the window, a sturdy door. Alex looked at the stone mullioned window and then at the ground beside it.

In the short, wiry grass was a small pile of pink and red matter. Alex's heart started pounding like a steam hammer. He heard Hex's voice as if from a long way off. 'Alex, they're deer entrails. Something's had a go at them, but they're from a deer.'

Hex was worried. Alex was clenching his fists, the knuckles white, his forehead grinding into the stone wall. Was he having a flashback? Hex reached out and touched him gently on the shoulder. 'Alex?'

Alex looked down at the little pile on the ground. He breathed out slowly to calm himself. Look at what's actually there, he said to himself. He'd seen animal entrails enough times not to be shocked by them. There were the intestines – a greyish pink curl with kinks like unravelled knitting. Those were the snakes. There was the heart – half eaten, and definitely not beating. There was a corner of the liver – most of it had gone but enough of its shiny lobes remained to show him why he had thought it was lips. And the kidneys, surrounded by white fat. That was what he'd thought was eyes.

'The people you saw were probably just game-keepers gutting a deer.'

Alex ran a hand wearily through his hair. 'No,

there was something else.' He sighed. 'I just can't remember it.'

Hex pressed his face to the window and cupped his hands around his eyes. 'Quite cosy in here.'

Alex looked too. Once again he was transported back to the previous night. There were things he'd seen but not particularly noticed: the fireplace, dusted with the remains of old fires; the pile of wood to the left-hand side of it; the oil lamp on the simple wooden table; the rough low benches; the washing line stretched across the room for drying wet clothes.

Hex moved to the door. 'Might as well have a look inside.' He tried the latch but the door wouldn't move. He looked down at the latch. Underneath it was a keyhole. 'It's got a lock.'

Alex joined him. 'It shouldn't have. The door's probably reclaimed from another building.' He put his thumb on the latch and pushed but the door didn't budge. He frowned and looked at Hex. 'These are supposed to be open so that anyone can use them.'

Hex stepped back and looked at the building.

'Maybe it's private property.' He walked round. Perhaps there was a sign or a notice they'd missed.

Around the other side, they found one:

GLAICKVULLIN ESTATE

THIS BOTHY IS ALWAYS UNLOCKED AND CAN BE USED

BY ANY PASSING TRAVELLER

PLEASE LEAVE IT AS YOU FIND IT

Alex looked at Hex. 'Then why is it locked?' A thought occurred to him and he gripped Hex's arm. 'Hex, I saw something weird last night and I can't quite remember it. It's like a radio station that's just out of tune – I can't get it but I know it's there. What if it was a murder? A dead body being cut up? There was definitely blood. And now they've locked the bothy so no one can get in and look around.'

'Alex, think,' said Hex. 'Do you really believe you saw a murder? If so, we'd better go to the police.'

Alex kicked the wall in frustration. 'I saw *something*. I just can't remember what.'

Hex led him round to the window again. 'Look in there. See if there's any sign of a murder. Personally,

I think there would be a hell of a mess: they'd have to hose the place down. But there's dust on the windowsill and ash and mud all over the floor. No one's cleaned that place up for a long time.' He looked at Alex. 'I think all you saw was a couple of gamekeepers working late.'

Alex sighed. 'I suppose so.'

Hex got out his palmtop. 'Let's see where Tiff's taken the others.'

'I'm lost,' said Tiff, and stopped, as though she had run out of steam.

They had been walking for two hours. Paulo had thought it would be good to let Tiff do the navigation. If she found walking boring, maybe she needed a mental challenge. So he, Li and Amber had followed her, patiently going where she took them, letting her make the decisions. Normally on an orienteering exercise they would stop frequently and check the map and the compass. But for the last twenty minutes Tiff hadn't looked at the map at all.

Now she stopped and said she was lost. The map

in its waterproof see-through cover swung around her neck. She made no attempt to look at it.

For heaven's sake, thought Amber, she couldn't be lost. All she had to do was look around. Behind was a river, crossed by a solid stone bridge. Beyond was a steep hillside of purple heather. It should be easy to spot such a distinctive combination of features on the map.

'Remember what I told you,' said Paulo patiently. 'First you set the map.'

'What's that?' Tiff's voice was flat, bored.

'Work out which way up the map should be,' said Li.

Tiff held the map up. 'It's got to be this way up, otherwise the writing will be upside down.'

Amber would have found it funny, but she was too annoyed at Tiff's obstructiveness. 'Look for the point where the bridge crosses the river,' she muttered.

Tiff looked at the map, then looked accusingly at Amber. 'There are two bridges.'

Li pointed behind them. 'Look for that hill.'

'There isn't anything marked "hill".

'Look for the contour lines,' said Paulo patiently.

Amber could see that Tiff was about to ask what those were and couldn't bear to hear such a stupid question. 'The red swirly lines,' she said. 'If they're close together, the land is steep. Look for tight contour lines on the north bank of the river, near a bridge.'

'Right,' said Tiff, her mouth working. She still didn't look at the map. 'And?'

'Now tell me the grid reference.'

Instead of answering, Tiff held out the map to Paulo to do it for her. His face looked like thunder.

Li wanted to giggle. She was always teasing laid-back Paulo about being lazy, and here he was being wound up by someone whose laziness was truly phenomenal.

But Paulo didn't see the funny side. 'Forget it,' he snapped. 'How did you get to the rave if you can't read a map?'

Tiff played the innocent. 'Why? Do you wanna dance?'

Amber tried to bring her back to the job in hand. 'Tiff, you said we're lost. How are you going to find out where we are?'

Tiff looked around and spotted a couple walking slowly along the riverbank; they were wearing gaiters and walking boots and carrying ski sticks. 'I'm going to ask those people for directions,' she said. As she approached them, a white pointer dog came bounding out of the foaming water. It sniffed around Tiff's feet and leaped on ahead.

'I am so looking forward to handing over to Alex and Hex,' muttered Paulo. 'I definitely need a run to get this out of my system.' They had planned to swap activities at a halfway point.

Amber watched Tiff show her map to the couple. 'I have never had to ask for directions anywhere,' she said through gritted teeth. 'I want the ground to open up and swallow me.'

The pointer sniffed at Paulo's feet and scooted off to the scrubby heather. He watched him, smiling.

The woman looked up and saw the dog. 'Pip!' she called. The dog looked up obediently.

Then there was a sudden blur of movement and the dog let out a yelp.

Paulo's head snapped round. That sounded bad. He dashed towards him, but as he skidded to his knees beside him, the pointer staggered and collapsed. Amber and Li hurried up to see what was going on.

Paulo had seen the scenario before, on the ranch: the sudden flurry of movement, the agonized cry. 'He's been bitten by a snake,' he told them.

8

MERCY MISSION

The couple ran over to their dog, with Tiff trailing behind them, but Li put her hands out to stop anyone going near the bush. 'Let the snake get away or it might attack again,' she told them.

'Snake?' repeated the middle-aged man, who had a ginger beard and a weathered face.

As Li watched the bush, she saw a dark shape flash away, curling like a snapping whip. It had a distinct zigzag marking like a tyre tread. 'It's an adder. It's poisonous.'

The woman clutched her husband's arm. 'Poisonous?'

'What do we do?' said Tiff.

Paulo had his hand on the dog's side, feeling the lungs under the smooth white hide. They were pumping hard and his breath rasped in his throat. Paulo looked up at the couple. 'Do you know where the nearest vet is?'

The woman shook her head. 'No, we're here on holiday.'

Li was already on her phone. 'Directory enquiries? I need an emergency vet, near to—' She grabbed the map hanging around Tiff's neck. 'Nearest to Vullin Lane, where it crosses Glaick River.' She dropped the map and waggled her fingers at Amber, as if dialling on a keypad.

Amber held up her phone. As Li listened to the number she punched it in on the mobile. Then Amber took over and called the vet.

'Hi, we've got an emergency – a dog has been bitten by an adder.'

Paulo didn't like the look of the dog's face. It was starting to swell, the flesh starting to balloon off the narrow skull. The dog's mouth was open, the tongue hanging out in a pink curl.

'Right. Thanks,' said Amber. She cut the call. 'Tiff, give me the map. There's a vet visiting the hunting lodge just down here. His receptionist is warning him we're on our way.'

Never taking her eyes off the dog, Tiff pulled the map case over her head and gave it to Amber.

Paulo scooped up the dog in his arms and staggered to his feet. He was a substantial weight, like a twenty-kilo sack of horse feed.

Amber inspected the map. 'Should be five minutes' walk.'

Paulo hoped five minutes wouldn't be too long. The dog was making a rasping noise as he breathed. That meant his airway was swelling already. Paulo set off at a run. The whole group followed, but Tiff and the couple slowed to a walk after twenty seconds, gasping.

Amber, still jogging alongside Li, turned round to call back to them, 'Meet us there. Glaickvullin Lodge.' And she sprinted on ahead of Paulo.

It was a single-track road, a straightforward route, but uphill. The dog was heavy and Paulo's biceps were soon on fire, but one look at the swollen head and the look of trust in the dog's brown eyes gave him the strength to go on. Maybe they could flag down a lift if a car came.

The dog's breathing was becoming more ragged. Paulo didn't know the exact effect of adder venom, but he knew one thing: as the dog's breathing got louder, his airway was getting smaller. Soon he would suffocate.

Moments later Amber came back, waving her arms like a semaphore messenger. 'It's just around this corner,' she called.

Paulo's thighs and biceps were burning, but Amber's news gave him the determination he needed. He put on a final spurt and was rewarded with a fairytale apparition: a nineteenth-century baronial castle looking out over a wide expanse of green pasture. Glaickvullin Lodge.

But Paulo didn't have time to take in the sights. He saw a drive leading off the road, around the side of the building.

Amber sprinted away, came back and beckoned. 'Follow the drive round the back,' she yelled. 'There's a yard with agricultural buildings.'

Paulo's feet crunched on fine gravel, slipped, but on he went. He passed a red Land Rover and glimpsed boxes of drugs and dressings in the back. Veterinary equipment. Then a man in a green surgical-looking coat rushed towards him, his arms out. Paulo handed Pip over, then bent over double, recovering. Li came alongside him and rubbed his back while Amber went with the vet in case he had any questions. Were they in time?

The vet put Pip gently on the ground and shone a pen torch in his eyes and mouth. 'Are you the owners?' he asked. In his top pocket were two syringes. He discharged one after the other into the dog's neck. He was well prepared.

'No, they'll be here any minute,' said Amber. Paulo and Li joined her, Paulo still breathing hard.

The vet felt Pip's face carefully. 'Do you know where the bite is?'

'We didn't see it,' said Li. 'He went off into a bush and—'

'Here it is,' said the vet. His fingers framed two garnets of blood on the side of the dog's jaw. A double puncture mark.

Li was looking towards the drive. 'Here are the owners,' she said and waved at the three figures approaching.

For the first time the friends noticed their surroundings. The place smelled comforting, of grain and farmyards. Two men wearing green tweeds were steadily sweeping the concrete yard. They must be gamekeepers; Alpha Force had seen a number of them out on the moors during the previous week.

Pip's owners rushed up to the vet. 'How is he?' panted the woman.

The vet got to his feet. 'He's stable for now but I need to take him into the clinic and put him on a drip.'

The woman gasped. Her husband put his arm around her. 'There is an antidote, isn't there?'

Tiff watched with big, horrified eyes.

The vet went to the back of his Land Rover and threw the discarded syringes in a special container. 'The poison isn't the problem. It's the swelling and the possibility of infection. Plus he's in shock. But you got him here just in time. Have you got a car here?'

The man shook his head. 'No, we were out walking. We're staying at the B&B in the village.'

'I'll take him in my Land Rover.' He looked at the group. 'But I can only take two passengers.'

Tiff stepped back from the couple. 'I'm not with them. I was just helping.'

The vet called to a gamekeeper, who was walking past with a broom. 'Rob, do you have an old feed sack I can put him on?'

The gamekeeper nodded. 'No problem.' He went off into a long outbuilding with a row of open doors. Just beyond were high fences of wire netting.

Now that the emergency was over Paulo had time to be curious. 'What animals do they have here?'

'Those pens are for pheasants,' replied the vet. 'They breed them for release at the start of the shooting season. They've got a few Highland cattle in pastures further up the moor.'

Amber and Li were more interested in the lodge itself. It was magnificent. Fawn-coloured stone walls topped with crenellations, square towers at each end, a small hexagonal folly rising out of the far tower with a flagpole on top.

'Nice place,' said Amber.

'Very nice,' agreed the vet. He lowered his voice. 'Very exclusive. Eight hundred quid a night. Keep your eyes open and you'll see some A-list celebrities.'

Well, thought Paulo, that might explain why that other gamekeeper over there has stopped sweeping and is staring at us. He must be checking us out to see if we're famous. Paulo gave him a wave. The man didn't respond, but stole a glance at them from time to time as he swept.

Rob came back and handed a large flattened cardboard box to the vet, who opened the Land Rover and spread it on the back seat. Then he suddenly noticed a label on the box. 'Rob, where did you get this?' He held out the cardboard flap so that the gamekeeper could see the label.

Rob read it out: '*Ketamine.*' He sounded unfamiliar with the word. He looked at the vet. 'Pesticides aren't my department.'

The vet shook his head. 'It's not a pesticide. You have to get it from a vet.'

Rob shrugged. 'You're the only vet we've had up here.'

'Your bosses haven't been getting veterinary drugs from somewhere else, have they?'

Rob shook his head. 'No, I don't think so.'

'Well, don't,' said the vet. 'They may be cheap but they're illegally imported and sometimes they don't even contain the drug you think you're buying.' Then he noticed the expectant faces around him. 'Sorry, lecture over. Let's get the dog in.'

Paulo realized that the second gamekeeper was still watching them. Still not quite sure, eh? he thought. Who do I look like? Enrique Iglesias?

Hex and Alex strode up the drive just as Pip's owners were putting the dog gently into the Land Rover. Hex had been tracking the other party on his palmtop.

Paulo went up to Alex. 'You look a lot better than you did this morning.'

Alex nodded. 'All I needed was a good run.'

Hex peered at the prostrate dog in the back of the Land Rover. The vet was making final checks on his pulse and breathing. 'What have you been up to here?'

'A bit of lifesaving,' said Paulo. 'All part of the entertainment for our guest.'

The vet started to shut the back door, but the flap of the cardboard box was in the way. Rob went over and tried to tear it but it was too tough, so Alex cut it off with his knife.

'Cheers.' The vet shut the door and climbed into the driver's seat; the middle-aged couple got in next to him.

'No problem,' said Alex, and he and Rob stepped away as the Land Rover's V8 engine roared into life.

Across the yard, Alex saw another gamekeeper leaning on a broom and staring at him. That's strange, he thought. Why is he looking at me like that? Then he told himself not to be so paranoid.

Li, Amber and Tiff came over. 'We'd better be going,' said Amber. 'More miles to cover.' They turned and started to walk down the drive.

Alex heard a voice beside him: 'Excuse me.' It was the gamekeeper with the broom. 'I'll take that.'

Alex had forgotten he was holding the piece of cardboard.

'I'm going to make a bonfire,' said the man. He had pale blue eyes and his face was scarred with acne pockmarks and a line like a neat cut on his cheek.

There's definitely something strange about him, thought Alex. He looked at the piece of cardboard, as if sizing it up, then pulled his rucksack off his back. 'If you're going to burn it, can I keep it? My quad bike's got an oil leak and I need to catch the drips.'

'I can get you another,' said the man. His blue eyes took on a steely glint.

Now Alex really was determined to keep the cardboard. 'No, this'll do fine.' He put it away.

The gamekeeper gave Alex a hostile stare and walked off.

As Rob accompanied them to the gate, a green Range Rover swung in from the lane. On the roof were three gutted deer carcasses. The five friends glimpsed shiny long black rifle barrels and tweed jackets. The driver pulled up and four figures got out. Their Highland tweeds were accessorized with funky scarves and swinging earrings.

'Hey, guys,' hissed Li. 'Do you know who that was? That R'n'B star. What's her name?' She narrowed her eyes, trying to remember.

Amber peered over Hex's shoulder. 'Well, whoever it is, green's not her colour.'

'Those people with the pointer should be very grateful to you,' said Rob. 'I had a gun dog which died from an adder bite. I was out on the moors with her; didn't get back quickly enough and she suffocated.'

Paulo was already jogging down the road backwards. 'No problem. Let us know if you get any news about him. We're staying at the hostel.'

'I will,' nodded Rob.

Li and Amber gave Alex and Hex a brief wave, then joined Paulo jogging down the road. Hex and Alex would take Tiff for the afternoon.

'We'd better be getting on too,' said Hex. 'We've got a walk ahead of us.' Tiff gave him a mutinous look, which he ignored.

A thought occurred to Alex. He called to Rob, who was walking back up the drive, 'Does anyone round here hunt at night?'

Rob shook his head. 'No. It's too dangerous to shoot in low visibility.'

Alex frowned. 'Not ever?'

'Not even the gamekeepers do it. Those rifle bullets travel a long way.' He waved to them. 'See you around.' He turned and walked back to the yard.

Alex frowned. If the gamekeepers weren't shooting at night, what were they doing out in the bothy so late?

9

SUSPICIONS

Tiff was on the phone. 'It's pants here. The rave was good but I'm fed up now.'

Hex caught a snatch of her conversation as he went past her room. 'Not as fed up as we are,' he muttered under his breath and headed down the stairs.

He found the others in the office – Alex sitting at the desk, Li perched on top of the filing cabinet, Paulo in one of the easy chairs and Amber cross-legged on the floor with the Ordnance Survey map. They were going to discuss the programme for the next day, but Alex had the piece of cardboard in front of him and was looking at the label.

'Hex, have you heard of ketamine?'

Hex sighed. 'So that's what you were fretting about all the way back.'

'I wasn't fretting, I was thinking,' said Alex.

Amber fixed Hex with a long-suffering expression. 'Hex, for goodness' sake do a search, tell him they use it to clean the silver and then we can get on with some planning.'

Hex had his palmtop switched on, the screen monitoring Tiff's position. So long as she was on the phone they knew where she was. He minimized that website screen and flipped open another to search. Seconds later, he had some results. '*Ketamine. Powerful anaesthetic used mainly on farm animals by vets. Also used by the rave subculture . . . known as Special K, Ket, Vitamin K or just K. Can cause hallucinations, or loss of co-ordination—*'

'Hallucinations?' repeated Alex.

Hex typed a couple more words into the search engine and scanned the results. 'It might be what you were given, but it's not the only thing that causes hallucinations.'

But Alex wouldn't let it go. 'Yet they do have ketamine at the lodge and Amber says the vet didn't prescribe it. Where did they get it?'

Hex's fingers worked again. He read the results. 'It's not illegal to possess it, but its sale and supply are controlled so it's illegal to give it away or sell it.' He looked up. 'They're not breaking any laws by having it.'

Alex still wasn't satisfied. 'What do they use it for? Why would they need to anaesthetize their animals?'

Paulo stepped in. 'You can use some anaesthetics as tranquillizers. It's very handy when you've got a tonne of heifer trying to kill you for treating a cut on her leg.'

Alex thought. 'What about that guy? The other gamekeeper?' He picked up the ketamine label between his thumb and forefinger. 'Did you see the way he looked at me when I wouldn't give this to him?'

Li was starting to get irritated. Surely Alex must realize he was making a mountain out of a molehill? He must still be a bit drugged. She had a point she wanted to make but she was afraid it would make Alex worse.

'That guy was looking at everyone,' said Paulo. 'He thought I was Enrique Iglesias.'

The room erupted in a gale of raucous laughter. Even Alex forgot his preoccupations and clutched the chair, helpless.

Hex calmed down first, tried to get the conversation back on track, but started chuckling instead, which set everyone off again. Gradually their mirth subsided.

Li felt a lot better. Paulo had cleverly cleared the air. 'Listen,' she said, 'didn't the vet say there was a drugs black market? Maybe that suspicious guy got the ketamine a bit cheap for general use around the animals and was trying to hide the fact.' She glanced at Paulo. 'What do you think, Enrique?'

Amber began chuckling again, then Paulo. That started Hex and Alex and before they knew it they were all helpless again.

Amber wiped a tear from her eye. 'Alex, just get this out of your system. Why don't you go and look at the bothy again now? There are enough of us here to sort out the kayaking gear for tomorrow. Go and do what you need to do.'

Li felt mean for being irritated with him earlier. 'I'll come with you,' she said. 'Kayaking's not my thing. I feel like another walk.'

Li and Alex climbed into the hills just as the sun was setting. The clouds had turned to purple and crimson; the mountains stood out black against a golden halo, as though there was a glowing fire just behind them. The two friends carried torches but preferred to keep them switched off, soaking up the silence, the vast purpling sky, the fresh cooling air. An owl rose out of the trees, its wings a wide silhouette, silent as a glider.

'This is so lovely,' said Li. 'What a pity people come here to kill things. That lodge rears pheasants and grouse for people to kill. And that pop star, or whoever she was, was out shooting deer today – who'd want to shoot a deer?'

'I suppose people pay a lot of money to hunt,' said Alex.

'They do in that place,' said Li. 'You know what

annoys me, it's not necessary. It's not like some of the parts of the world we've been to, where you have to be self-sufficient. If we were in the middle of the jungle and we had to kill something to get a meal, I've no problem with that. But a bunch of rich Hooray Henrys – they can't eat a whole deer and they probably wouldn't want to.'

They started to climb more steeply, pulling themselves up on rocks that jutted out of the wiry grass. 'Have you seen Glaickvullin village?' said Alex.

'No.'

'I saw it last week when I took Amber down to get more insulin.' Amber was a diabetic and had to take regular medication, but she didn't let it cramp her style.

'And?' said Li.

'Well, you know Tongue?'

'Yes.' Tongue was a tiny village; they went there to get petrol and diesel for the vehicles. Aside from the petrol station it had a hotel, a bank, a farm and some cottages. That was all.

'Glaickvullin's like a different planet,' said Alex.

'How?'

They reached the top of the hill. Below, the white walls of the hostel reflected the sunset glow.

'It's got a posh country clothing shop and a gift shop selling lots of things marked WITH LOVE FROM SCOTLAND. There are a lot of local people making a living out of the people who come here to shoot. And then there are the gamekeepers – it's a traditional job. They have to look after the environment, farming the heather, making sure the animals on the estate are healthy . . .'

Li paused, hands on hips. 'But they shoot so many birds they have to keep rearing more of them or they'd die out.'

'Many more of them are released than are shot. A lot of them go and live in the wild.'

They marched on again. 'That doesn't make sense, Alex. If there are a lot of them in the wild, why do the keepers have to breed them?'

'Too many natural predators. And the weather's so cold up here that partridge and pheasant don't breed. The point is, it's a natural resource, like oil. The gamekeepers make sure it's managed in a responsible, sustainable way.'

'You sound like you've been finding out a lot about this.'

'My mum has. She doesn't want me to have a job where I might get shot at, like my dad. My careers officer told her about gamekeeping and she thought it would be perfect – the outdoors, and a few guns, but—'

'But nice and safe. Birds and deer can't shoot back.'

'Precisely,' said Alex. 'She's worried I'm going to try for the armed forces again.' Some time ago Alex had applied to join the army but had been turned down. He'd been gutted, but he'd never quite let go of the dream.

They walked on. Instead of wiry grass swishing against their legs they felt brittle twigs which smelled charred. The gamekeepers had been out burning heather, which kept it in good condition to provide cover for the birds.

'Parents, huh?' said Li. 'Always trying to wrap you in cotton wool.'

'Yeah,' said Alex. 'Can't be easy for Mum, though. She gets so worried about Dad. Hey – were you checked out by the police before this trip? To see if you had any criminal history before they let you look after the kids?'

Li nodded. 'Yeah. I was dead scared what they'd turn up. All these things we've done over the past few years – I know it wasn't illegal but I'd hate my parents to know about it.'

Alex agreed. 'I was scared stiff until they gave me the all-clear.' He turned his torch on to check his compass. It was fully dark now; the torch would have to stay on.

'So what does the future hold for you, Li?'

'I have an uncle with a traditional martial arts school in Shanghai.'

Alex asked, half joking, 'Is there a Cheong style of martial arts?'

'Actually there is. There are thousands of traditional family styles of martial arts throughout the country.'

'And might the Cheong academy be getting a dynamic new sensei?'

Li sighed. 'I don't know. I'd really, really like to carry it on. They all say I'm the natural successor, but I don't know if I'm ready to settle down.'

Settle down. The words made Alex feel sad.

Li stopped and shone the torch around. 'Hey,' she whispered. The beam caught a stone wall twenty metres away.

'That's it,' said Alex.

They crept up in silence. The bothy was dark. Alex's torch reflected off the windows in a white slick. He peered inside. It all looked much the same as earlier that day.

Li tried the door. 'Locked.'

Alex stood back and shone his torch over the building. It looked peaceful and quiet, like an empty house.

Li went and stood close to him. 'What now?'

'I feel like a right twit. But I'd like to stay for a bit, see if anything happens.'

There was a low stone wall that went round one side of the bothy, like a garden wall. They sat down beside it, huddling into the shadow. The two friends could have carried on their conversation, but now things were different. This was a mission.

After about ten minutes a new sound joined the peaceful night sounds. At first it was barely noticeable, like a buzzing insect, but bit by bit it became louder. An engine. Coming their way.

Li gripped Alex's arm. Two pinpoints of light bounced up the hill. Headlights.

Alex's mind raced. He hadn't expected a vehicle – by the sound it must be a quad bike; he'd thought it would be somebody on foot. Had there been a vehicle the previous night? There could have been, parked behind the bothy.

Would the driver see them in the headlights? They hadn't come kitted out for camouflage. Alex's combat trousers were khaki, which looked pale at night. Why hadn't he worn black? They hadn't got camouflage cream on either. 'Hide your face,' he hissed to Li.

The bike pulled up beside the bothy and the engine stopped. A torch flashed around, then a figure was at the door. The lock clicked and the hinges creaked open. A shadow passed inside, its footsteps like sandpaper on the gritty floor inside. There was a golden flare as a match was lit, followed by a softer glow that lit the room gently. The paraffin lamp.

A second figure remained on the bike, a cigarette

glowing red and lighting up his hands. The acrid tang of the smoke drifted over to Li and Alex. He was only ten metres away from them. They stayed very, very still. The other figure came back out of the bothy. The lighted cigarette was mashed under a boot. Then they both went inside.

Li and Alex could see the pale square of light on the ground, occasionally darkened by shadows moving across the window. It allowed them to make out the vehicle – a six-wheeled all-terrain vehicle, or ATV, similar to the quad bikes they had at the hostel.

Li decided it was safe to whisper. 'Should we go closer—?'

Suddenly the door opened and the two figures came out again. A deer carcass swung heavily between them. They loaded it onto the flat bed at the back of the ATV, went back in, then came out with another. Their torches illuminated the name on the flat bed: 6x6 POLARIS, and a dent in the flange of metal that arched over the wheel. One of the men pulled elastic ropes over the carcasses to secure them while the other went back into the bothy. The pale square of light in the window disappeared, leaving only the pinpoint of torches. The door was locked, then the engine chugged into life and the headlights came on. The second man climbed on behind the driver and they sped away, the headlights questing into the night.

Li and Alex breathed out a long, grateful sigh. Alex got up and looked through the window of the bothy, shining his torch in.

'Anything?' said Li, coming up behind him.

'Can't see much,' said Alex. He turned to look at her. 'But Rob at the lodge specifically said nobody went shooting at night.'

'There wasn't any shooting,' said Li. 'Those deer were already dead. The guys were probably catching up with work.'

Alex searched the ground with his torch. 'You always gut them immediately they're shot. If you leave them they blow up with gas and smell awful. And I can't see any entrails here.'

'So those deer were already gutted.'

'But that's weird,' said Alex agitatedly. 'Those people who went shooting this morning had their carcasses with them to show off their catch.' He looked at Li, who was standing with her hands on her hips. Her body language was saying 'sceptical'. Alex sighed. 'I'm going off on one again, aren't I?'

Li prodded him gently in the ribs. 'At least they showed up. You didn't imagine it entirely. However, I was expecting them to do something a bit more exciting.'

Alex turned away from the bothy. 'Come on, let's get back.'

For a while they walked in silence. Li could tell that Alex was lost in his thoughts. Although he was trying to laugh it off now, there was something still bothering him. Whatever he thought he saw here must have been quite upsetting. She'd heard that people who had a bad trip on LSD could be deeply scarred. In a way, she understood. She'd had a bad experience abseiling once, and it took her a long time to put it behind her. Perhaps it was a similar feeling.

'Go on,' she said, 'tell me what you're thinking. I know you're still fretting.'

Alex sighed. 'I just keep thinking there's something important I've forgotten.'

Li's torch picked out a shiny object in the darkness. She stopped, startled. Her voice dropped to a whisper. 'That wasn't there before.'

They went closer. Their torches picked out six tyres, shiny green paintwork, handlebars. The name on the flat bed: 6x6 POLARIS. The same dent in the wheel arch.

'It's the ATV from the bothy,' whispered Li. 'What's it doing here?'

Alex put his hand on the bonnet. It was warm, but had probably been stopped for about five minutes. Li flashed her torch around. There was no sign of the drivers. She peered into the darkness for torches, but the night was pitch black.

Alex inspected the flat bed on the back of the ATV. 'The deer are gone. But where are the drivers?'

Li looked at the map. She laughed quietly.

'What's funny?'

'Oh it's nothing.' She felt silly. Then she felt dishonest. Here was Alex, trying to get to grips with a weird experience; the least she could do was confess about her own. 'You know the cave where Tiff got stuck and I had to rescue her? The cave with the noise?'

'Yeah.'

'Well, the more I thought about it, the more I was convinced it sounded like a generator. When we got back I got out the map of the pothole and matched it up with the Ordnance Survey map. I really was thinking there might be a machine buried in a hidden cave there, doing something clandestine. But it was just open moor.'

Alex shrugged. 'Maybe what you heard was somebody driving nearby. Or an underground water course.'

'No, it didn't sound like that. It was constant, but it didn't really sound like water. Paulo came in while I was looking and asked what I was doing. I pretended I was looking at the map for another reason. Anyway, just as a matter of interest, it was right here. And now here's the *Mary Celeste* ATV.'

Alex chuckled and linked his arm through hers. 'Glad I'm not the only one going mad. Come on, let's get back. Thanks for coming out with me.'

10

WHALE

A grey seal swam alongside Paulo's kayak, its dark eyes looking at him curiously, its long snout ending in two narrow nostrils. It had been following them since they pushed off from the stony shore.

A road bridge crossed high above them, making a dark shadow across the choppy water. Six yellow Day-Glo kayaks paddled out of the V-shaped inlet, on their way to the sea – Amber and Hex at the front, Alex and Tiff in the middle and, bringing up the rear, Li and Paulo. Plus one seal.

Paulo grinned at it, gliding with the current, not

wanting to put his paddle in the water in case he hurt it. His hair had gone especially wild in the sea spray, wiry like the seal's whiskers, thought Li. What was it with him? Animals always seemed to like him.

Beyond the bridge the shores opened out and the water merged with the sea. Far behind, the village looked like a small collection of white dolls' houses, the ruined castle that stood on the bluff a tiny double prong of brickwork. Gulls and cormorants soared in the thermals, calling to each other.

The only other sound was the splash of oars. The kayaks were perfect for seeing the wildlife in the open water – they made hardly any wake, unlike a motorized vessel, and were safer than swimming.

Suddenly the sound of the birds multiplied by a thousand. The clear blue sky was full of black shapes, swooping towards a point on the rocky coastline. Alex was reminded of his grandmother in Sunderland: she used to put out chicken scraps on the patio, and what seemed like a hundred birds appeared from nowhere and dived onto the little garden. There must be a freshly dead animal over there, he thought – perhaps a sheep had fallen from the cliff. His gaze drifted that way.

It was a boat, being loaded by a couple of figures. Fishermen? They were swinging a heavy load into the boat. At first Alex thought it was a tarpaulin full of fish. Then he caught a glimpse of a delicate head, fine legs. Deer carcasses.

He watched them go in. One. Then another. Three altogether. There was another man in the boat; he pulled a big tarpaulin over the carcasses.

Li had seen it too. She tried to alert Paulo but he was still teasing the seal as the boat pulled away. The birds followed a little way, but gradually dispersed. The two men walked back inland and disappeared behind a rock. The boat put on a burst of speed: even Paulo looked up at the sound of it. It sped out round the coast to the east.

Suddenly a louder noise claimed Li's attention. A rumble underneath her, like water coming to the boil. One moment she was up in the air, the next she was falling face first into dark blue water. The cold closed around her head like an iron vice.

But her reactions were well honed: she twisted

and the kayak rolled right over. As she came up and shook her head, blinking salt water out of her eyes, she saw Paulo treading water beside his kayak, his arms around it like a big drum, his lifejacket like two orange pillows at his ears. The seal was still beside him, a snout and eyes bobbing up and down on the same wave as Paulo. It looked like an earless Labrador.

'Look,' called Amber. 'Quick!'

A plume of water rose from the choppy surface, showering them in fine mist. The water slid away to reveal a giant curved tail. It waved gracefully in the air, a massive, black, barnacle-encrusted tower, the height of a small building. It slid back into the water with a splash, leaving a small swirling current. A humpback whale.

Tiff's kayak was thrown against Alex's. He looked at her quickly and mouthed, *OK?* She nodded.

Li, Hex and Amber looked around for Paulo. He was still in the water – had he been dragged down when the whale submerged? But no, there he was, hanging onto his kayak. He heaved himself up with his arms and folded his long legs back into the vessel. He pulled up the plastic skirt that kept the water out around his waist, and the seal spooked and scooted away.

Amber saw out of the corner of her eye a network of white bubbles on the surface, like a lace doily. It was the whale's blowhole. She glanced at Hex. 'Get outta here!' she yelled. The two friends paddled like mad in different directions. Moments later the whale exploded onto the surface, drenching them.

Hex stopped paddling and looked back. From the side the whale's mouth was like two giant mussel shells, its dark glossy back like a small submarine as it arced through the water. Beyond, Amber bobbed on the water like a doll in a shoe. The whale slipped into the water again.

The kayakers watched the water, enchanted, poised to flee if the whale came up again. But the water remained still. The whale had gone.

Ahead was a small island, a rocky hump about ten kilometres long. It stuck out of the water like a tooth. Birds wheeled in the air above it and tiny figures moved on the rocky outcrops, as though the surfaces were covered in ants. Amber, as lead scout, pointed her oar towards it. That was where they were going.

Back in formation, they paddled closer. Bird lime streaked the cliffs like white paint, making the cracked grey rock underneath look forbidding. The island was covered in seals. A family of them humped awkwardly down a rocky incline into the water. They looked like people trying to crawl in sleeping bags, thought Amber. The moment they hit the water they transformed into torpedoes, their streamlined bodies looping up and down through the waves, their skin glistening like shiny rubber.

The kayaks picked up speed. The current was getting stronger as the sea became shallower, but Amber had expected this. An experienced sailor, she had planned the route so that a novice like Tiff could cope. She checked her wrist-mounted compass and led the group to the left, around the end of the island. Gannets soared off the cliffs above them.

Tiff shrieked. She pointed with her oar and Alex's head snapped round, looking for the danger. A small dorsal fin was slicing through the surface near Alex's boat.

'Shark!' she shouted, although most of the sound was lost in the cries of sea birds.

It wasn't a shark. Alex tried not to smile. He let go of one oar and mimed a dolphin swimming.

Tiff mouthed something at him in reply. He didn't bother to lip-read.

A dark hole appeared in the white-streaked rock. Amber adjusted her course so that they were heading straight for it. A cave. They paddled closer to the rocks. Little eddies of foam splashed up against them. Then they slipped inside the dark hole and the sound changed.

The roaring wind and the calling birds were muffled. Instead they could hear the soft splash of their paddles, the water lapping against the rock walls.

'Ah, peace and quiet,' sighed Amber. It was the first time they'd been able to talk.

'Where do we have lunch?' said Paulo. His curly hair was plastered to his head after his dunking.

At the end of the cave was a small sandy beach and a cluster of rocks. The group climbed out of their kayaks into the water and secured them carefully, then flopped down on the sand, stretched their cramped limbs and enjoyed freedom.

Amber crawled over to her kayak and pulled a waterproof bag out of the foot. 'Chocolate, guys?'

Paulo didn't need to be asked twice. As soon as Amber offered the bar of Galaxy his hand whipped it away. She passed another bar to Alex.

'Hope you haven't got any fish-paste sandwiches,' said Li. 'We could get pecked to death.'

Tiff refused the chocolate and popped a piece of gum into her mouth. 'Who's picking us up?'

'No one's picking us up,' said Alex. 'We're going back the way we came.'

'I can't,' said Tiff. 'I'm knackered.'

Amber didn't think Tiff looked any more tired than usual, just bored. She shouldn't have found the trip that taxing. 'You could wait for a passing ship,' said Amber coldly. 'Flag down a lift.' She was fed up with Tiff and her difficult moods.

'Have some chocolate,' said Hex, passing her a bar. 'It'll make you feel better.'

Amber got to her feet and went over to her kayak. She didn't need anything, she just wanted to get away from Tiff. Otherwise she might say something she'd regret. She pretended to inspect the kayak but instead she looked into the water as the waves rose up the little beach and withdrew again.

There was a shape in the water, coming towards the shore. In the gloom it was difficult to see it properly. As it came closer she caught a glimpse of eyes and a snout. She stood up. 'Hey, guys, I think there's an otter here.'

Li picked her way over and peered into the water. 'I can't see any movement,' she said.

The waves came up the beach and withdrew again. Again the glimpse of dark eyes, closer still. But it looked like it was drifting, not swimming. 'It's dead,' she said.

She picked up her paddle and reached into the water. A wave brought it close and she held it. She turned to the others. 'It's a deer.'

Alex got up and clambered over. 'A deer?' He remembered what he'd seen in what he thought was a fishing boat.

Li looked at the wet hide. There was a long

incision in the pale fur along its abdomen. It flapped open. 'And – uh – this is weird. It's been gutted.'

'Gutted?' repeated Amber.

Alex bent down and gingerly pushed the flap of skin aside.

Tiff shrieked. 'Ugh, you are gross.'

'Just checking,' he said, and carried on.

Inside was a big red cavity where the heart, lungs, liver and intestines had been.

'It's quite fresh,' said Alex.

'Well, it can't have been in the water long,' said Paulo, and popped a piece of chocolate into his mouth. 'The birds will have it in no time.'

'But where did it come from?' asked Hex.

'Sainsbury's,' muttered Tiff. 'Who cares?'

Li gave Alex a significant look. Alex knew what it meant. The boat they had seen earlier, taking delivery of deer carcasses.

'Conference later,' she said quietly. 'When we've got rid of Little Miss Muffet.'

'What are you whispering about?' said Tiff.

Li pushed the deer back out with her oar. 'Just saying a prayer while we bury this dead deer.'

Instead of floating out, the deer came back in. The waves deposited it at Tiff's feet. The head bobbed and touched the toe of her boot.

The friends stood, waiting for the tantrum. But Tiff simply kicked the deer's nose away. 'Dead things. In a cave on a desolate rock. What a surprise. I'm having such a good time here. When are we going?'

Amber looked out towards the cave mouth. Where before there had been a clear blue sky, there was now a wall of grey. 'Picnic over, guys. We'd better get back. It's got rather misty out there.'

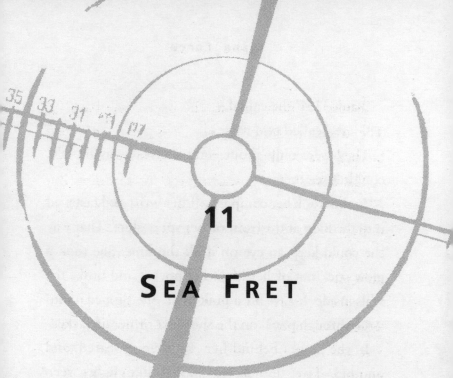

11

SEA FRET

'Keep to the middle of the channel, guys, in case there are rocks near the surface.' Amber led the group cautiously out of the caves. They paddled slowly, in single file.

One by one they slipped out into the open sea. Immediately the air sang with the cries of birds. Amber checked her compass. They were heading back towards the Kyle, the big inlet of water, but the massive bridge had vanished in the fog. She could see Hex beside her, and he could see Alex and Tiff behind, but she couldn't see anyone else.

'Paulo? Li?' she called.

'Here,' called two voices.

They were only about eight metres away but she couldn't see them.

Amber took her compass off her wrist and fastened it to the loop at the front of her spray skirt. That way she could keep an eye on it all the time. She took a glow stick out of her lifejacket pocket and broke the vials inside. It gave off a pink light. She slipped it into a see-through panel on the shoulder of her lifejacket.

In the gloom behind her, another appeared, and another. Five fluorescent blobs, like lights seen through opaque glass. OK, now she could see everyone. She just had to get them back.

She had navigated her parents' yacht through bad weather before, in the open sea – far further from land than this. But a yacht felt substantial. Right now she felt like she was sitting in a sleeping bag on the water. Any moment she expected the whale to heave up and capsize one of them again.

She put such thoughts out of her mind. She had to stay calm, give confident leadership. She paddled steadily, decisively. The others followed.

A bird loomed out of the mist and brushed against her shoulder, a heavy, fluttering shape. The shock nearly made her capsize. Behind, Tiff let out a cry.

'They're attracted by the glow sticks,' said Alex. 'They won't hurt you.'

Tiff let out a storm of expletives.

Alex's voice soared above the sound of the wind. 'Tiff, don't throw the glow stick away. If you fall in or drift away we could lose you.'

Amber glanced back. Tiff had the glow stick in her hand, about to throw it into the sea. Another bird buffeted against her and she cried out again.

A bird screeched next to Amber's ear. Her heart turned somersaults as wings brushed against her face and she wobbled crazily in her kayak. Somewhere behind her, Paulo and Alex were pleading with Tiff.

Amber recovered her balance, took a deep breath and checked her compass again. Just as she thought: a little off course. She adjusted, then looked behind to check the others were still there. Five eerie fluorescent blobs, like alien life forms. Good. Paulo and Alex had persuaded her.

Amber kept her strokes slow and sure, aware of every variation in the current. It would be so easy to drift, the fog was completely disorientating. 'Sea fret', that's what sailors called a mist like this. It was a good name.

Tiff paddled on. She couldn't see anything but acres of white, and the five shadowy figures of the others. Inside her was a cold, numb fear. In her mind's eye she saw the sea stretching endlessly away, with her floating helplessly like a speck of plankton. A bird swooped out of the whiteness like an arrow. She threw her arms up to protect her face, imagining hooked beaks and claws.

Somewhere dimly above her, Tiff heard a swish of car tyres on a wet road. 'Hey!' she yelled. 'I can hear cars!'

'It's the bridge,' said Alex beside her. He sounded so calm and confident. Tiff felt angry. Why had they brought her out kayaking if they knew something like this could happen? Another bird dive-bombed her. She clamped her lips shut and batted it away, determined not to scream. If they'd planned all this to frighten her, she wasn't going to give them the satisfaction of seeing her fear.

'Land!' There was a rasp as a kayak bit into the pebbled shore.

Thank goodness, thought Tiff. She splashed out into the water. It was freezing but she kept her complaints to herself.

'Are you OK, Tiff?' asked Paulo.

'Fine,' said Tiff, tight-lipped.

'You're doing really well.'

If this is some kind of test, thought Tiff, I'll make you regret it.

The beach was white and featureless, like the sea. 'Hey – where's the Range Rover?' asked Hex. He actually laughed. The steel in Tiff's heart hardened even further.

Amber put her compass back on her wrist. 'This way.'

They stowed their paddles in the kayaks and picked them up. Amber began to walk and the others followed her pink glow.

Tiff picked up the kayak. She could barely get her arm around it. Not like Paulo, who found it easy to carry because his arms were as long as a gorilla's. But they probably wanted her to stop and complain.

Her feet were slipping on the wet rocks, she was freezing cold and the sea birds still kept coming after her. She stopped and took her glow stick out of its see-through pocket.

'No, keep it,' said Li urgently. 'You might still get lost.'

Tiff put it back wordlessly. You really are going to regret this, she thought. Somehow I'll make you pay.

They reached a slope strewn with boulders. The group slowed, working their way up carefully. Tiff's kayak bumped on the rocks. She lost her footing and crashed to the ground. Her kayak boomed like a drum roll in a circus. She got laboriously to her feet, fuming, and picked it up again.

The others had got ahead already. Their glows were like a stain of candy fading into the liquid mist. 'Hey!' she shrieked.

'We're here,' called Paulo, glowing orange. 'Follow the lights. Are you all right?'

'Yes.' Tiff spoke through gritted teeth.

'Not far now,' said Alex. 'Just keep going.'

On they trudged again. The ground changed under her feet. Soft springy turf, not those slippery boulders. Suddenly something made an electronic chirruping noise. Two sets of orange lights flashed. Tiff nearly jumped out of her skin.

'Ah, there you are,' said Amber. Tiff heard a car door opening. They had found the Range Rover.

Tiff felt like sitting down and having a good cry. She had never been so frightened in her life.

Alex was carrying an armful of lifejackets in through the front door of the hostel when he heard a door slam emphatically upstairs.

Li, unlacing her boots in the arched porch, had heard it too. 'That's the bathroom, unless I'm very much mistaken. Think she's going to be a long time?' The mist was thinner up here. Li could see the others outside lifting kayaks and paddles down from the roof rack.

Alex smiled. 'Long enough for a conference.'

'I saw the men in the boat too,' said Paulo.

Amber tapped a pen on the desk, turning it over and over. 'Yeah, I wondered what they were up to.'

They didn't think Tiff would disturb them,

but just in case, they held their meeting in the office. Wetsuits had been swapped for T-shirts and shorts.

'You say they had deer?' said Hex. 'The carcass in the cave must have fallen out of that boat.'

'Would it have got into the cave in that time?' said Li.

'There was a strong current system,' said Amber. 'It could have been washed in quite easily.'

Paulo sat back in the easy chair. 'So it looks like there's poaching in the area.' He looked at Li and Alex. 'That explains why you've seen people behaving suspiciously.'

'Should we try and do anything?' said Li.

'Be careful who we run into,' grinned Paulo immediately.

The others laughed but they all understood the seriousness of his words. They had come up against poachers before in a game reserve in Zambia and had barely escaped with their lives.

'They're probably in a stinking mood too,' said Hex. 'They lost thirty per cent of their stock over the side this morning. I think we should drop a subtle hint with that gamekeeper we met yesterday and then make sure we don't run into them again.'

'Good plan,' said Amber. She looked at her watch. 'It's lunch time. What are we going to do with Miss Congeniality this afternoon?'

Paulo looked out of the window down the valley. 'The mist has cleared quite a lot. How about your rock climbing, Li?'

Li shook her head. 'No, it's up by the Kyle. It'll be too wet and slippery. We'd be better leaving that until another day.'

'OK, then,' said Paulo. 'There's the riding stables down at Glaickvullin. I'll phone them – how many are coming?'

Amber stood up. 'I'll sit this one out,' she said. 'Someone else go.'

Paulo looked surprised. Just the previous week the highlight for Amber was taking Fleur and Claire, two experienced riders, out for a gallop on the moors.

Amber got up and went to the door. 'It's my turn to cook tonight. I'll do something American while you guys are out.' As she passed Alex, she shook him gently by the shoulders. 'Alex, are you worrying about those poachers?'

'No,' said Alex, but he knew very well his face said yes.

Paulo was riffling through the phone book, looking for the number of the stables. 'It's just a few deer, Alex. If the poachers didn't shoot them the tourists or gamekeepers would.'

Alex nodded. 'I'll have a word with Rob at the lodge, when I take you guys down to the stables. He can decide if there's anything to worry about.' But something was nagging at the back of his mind. Poaching? Was that all it was? He didn't think so.

Hex followed Amber out to the kitchen. 'Giving up the prospect of riding? Are you feeling well?'

Amber picked up the cutlery tray and took it to the drawer. 'I'd love to go riding. I just don't want it ruined by her.'

Hex picked up some plates from the draining board and stacked them in the cupboard. 'She's really getting to you, isn't she?'

Behind him he heard the sound of cutlery crashing

together. He looked round. Amber was practically throwing the knives, forks and spoons into their trays. 'She's like a cloud of bad vibes. She hates everything. Everything's "minging". She hates our guts and I have a natural aversion to being around people who would gladly stab me in the back. I can't wait for the weekend.'

'Rich girl who hates the world? You know, she reminds me of someone I used to know.' Hex looked at Amber, dreading her response. The words had come out before he'd even thought about them.

Amber was standing facing the sink, her back to him. She was very, very still.

'OK,' said Hex. 'I'll take my punishment like a man. Execute me now.'

Amber pivoted on her heel. Her eye had a cold look in it. In her hand was a big, heavy frying pan. 'Ah,' he said. 'Death by cast-iron frisbee.'

But Amber didn't clobber him. She smiled. 'You're in luck. I nearly had a huge sense of humour failure, huh?' She passed him the pan.

Hex took it and put it away.

* * *

Alex drove out of the stable yard. In his rear-view mirror he could see Tiff waving her hand in front of her face, her nose wrinkled in disgust, while Paulo and Li talked to the yard manager. He was relieved to have a break from her for a while, too. He changed down a gear and headed up hill. The castellated turrets of Glaickvullin Lodge peeped out over the tops of the tall fir trees. Now the sun was out and its upper windows glinted like slivers of obsidian.

The road levelled out by the lodge gates. Coming down from the moors was a Land Rover marked GLAICKVULLIN LODGE, the carcass of a magnificent red stag tied to the roof rack. It was just about to turn in and Alex pulled onto the grass to give them room. As it came alongside he saw the face of the driver. It was Rob, the gamekeeper, and he had a passenger: a slim-built man in a checked shirt and a green waxed jacket.

Rob waved to Alex and braked. The head of the stag nodded with the impact, antlers drumming on the vehicle roof. The window slid down smoothly.

'Hi, Rob,' Alex called.

'I spoke to the vet today. That dog your friends rescued is going to be fine. The owners asked me to thank you.'

'That's great news,' said Alex. 'I'll pass it on.' He nodded at the beast on the roof. 'Looks like you've had a good day.'

The man in the passenger seat leaned forward and smiled. 'All thanks to my wonderful gamekeepers. They just tell me where to point the gun and I shoot. I'm Frank Allen, the laird. Everything all right up at the hostel?'

'Fine, thanks,' said Alex. 'Good facilities. Great area.' He waved to Rob and moved off. Better to wait until he could get Rob in private to mention their suspicions about the other gamekeeper. He didn't want to get Rob into trouble. Instead he swung the Range Rover up the hill. As he drove, his mind was gnawing away at something. The laird wasn't what Alex was expecting. His accent wasn't local; not even Scottish. More like London. And street London, not stockbroker London. Hex's kind of accent. There was more. Alex had taken in a lot about the man during their short meeting. His waxed jacket was brand new; it still had that glossy patina. Where Rob's had scuff marks, particularly on his right shoulder, from constant friction with the stock of a rifle, the laird's was pristine. Either he'd just bought it or he rarely went out shooting.

12

STRANGE CARGO

Li thought how funny it was to compare the riding styles of her two companions. Paulo rode with long reins, his hips swaying as he let the big ex-racehorse find her own way up the steep bridle path. Behind him, on a small, stocky piebald, Tiff sat very straight in the saddle, as though she was having a deportment lesson. Every now and then she would try to slouch, but when she forgot herself, she sat erect with her heels down and her reins short, making sure her pony was on the bit. It was funny to see her doing something properly for once, despite her conscious efforts not to. She had obviously learned to ride quite well.

Li preferred Paulo's style – hardly surprising, as he had been her teacher on vacations on his parents' ranch. He'd taught her to go with the horse's own sense of balance, and that was what she was doing now, her chestnut Arab finding her own path behind Tiff's Welsh cob.

They reached the top. A long stretch of grass lay ahead, running along a gently undulating ridge line. Paulo gathered up the reins, ready for a canter. Jess, his mount, pranced a few steps, knowing what was coming. Then two men in green tweeds appeared on the left-hand side of the ridge, leading a black pony with hairy legs like flared trousers. On the pony's back was a deer carcass, tethered to an adapted saddle with elastic rope. The deer's head moved in rhythm with the pony's steps.

Paulo squeezed the reins and calmed Jess's bouncy stride. They would have their canter later, once the other pony was well out of the way, otherwise they might upset it. Horses were herd animals and if one started galloping, the others tended to join in. He looked behind him. The other horses were under control, walking obediently.

Suddenly the pack pony stumbled. It lurched forwards, its hooves scrabbling to find a purchase. Instead of turf they found slippery rock. The pony lost its footing altogether and crashed to the ground. The gamekeepers yelled, startled. In moments the pony was on its feet and galloping straight at Paulo. He caught a glimpse of two white-rimmed, panicked eyes in a black face, like a little demon. It went past and Tiff's pony surged after it as if leaping out of the starting gates.

Jess jogged, eager to follow, but Paulo held her in. Tiff and the other pony were hurtling back towards the edge of the ridge they had just climbed. It was very steep and rocky and if they went down there at speed, they'd fall for sure.

Paulo eased the reins. Jess took off in pursuit, her ears fixed on the two rumps in front of her. Behind, Li's horse had joined the stampede.

In moments Jess passed Tiff's pony, then the little black draught pony. Paulo swerved in front of them, sat down firmly in the saddle and squeezed the reins.

But instead of slowing, Jess powered on. Paulo pulled sharply and the horse yanked back hard, still galloping. She didn't want to stop. She was winning the race.

The edge was three strides away. If he didn't stop, the others would follow him down and there would be an accident. Paulo relaxed his fingers, sat down hard and squeezed with his legs. Jess's weight shifted backwards. At that moment he turned the top half of his body and Jess suddenly found herself facing the oncoming horses. She stopped, puzzled.

Tiff's piebald cob saw the big mare ahead, stuck his heels in the turf and slid to a stop as did the little pack pony. Tiff went forwards onto his neck, but she didn't fall. Li's chestnut Arab ploughed into the group, but Li kept her balance.

Paulo heaved a sigh of relief. Crisis averted. 'Everyone OK?'

Li's eyes were dancing. He could see she had enjoyed every moment. Tiff was out of breath and didn't look amused as she pushed herself back off the horse's neck and into the saddle. The horses stood blowing, their sides heaving, their eyes bright. They loved a race.

'Good handbrake turn, Paulo,' said Li.

Jess put her head up and skipped on the spot. She was ready to go again. Paulo patted her. 'Yes, you won, old girl. Wish I could give you a proper race.'

But there were other things to do. The pack pony was standing a little way away, looking at Paulo, its eyes wide and wary. If it took off again, Jess would follow. He'd better catch it before it caused more chaos.

He dismounted. 'You two stay there.' He pulled Jess's reins over her head and handed them to Li, then walked towards the black pony. He kept his walk deliberately unhurried, his hands down, his posture unthreatening. The pony would be easily spooked. He talked softly, in the coaxing tones he used when soothing a nervous animal on the ranch. He could see the triangle of sweat on the pony's neck, the salmon-pink flesh inside the widened nostrils, the white rim around the eyes. The reins were broken, hanging down like uneven shoelaces. He could have made a grab for them, but instead he ran a reassuring hand down the pony's sweaty neck. Then he grasped the rein.

The pony flinched, but Paulo was ready with a

soothing word. It flicked an ear and slid its eye sideways, but relaxed. Paulo felt a few spots of rain, big, splashy drops. *Dios*, this Scottish weather, he thought. What next, a hurricane?

The green figures of the gamekeepers were running towards him. The pony saw them and flinched, but Paulo comforted it again. He put up his hand to tell the gamekeepers to slow down, but they took no notice. Paulo decided to walk the pony back to them. Maybe then they would stop running, which was only upsetting it.

They slowed to a walk as Paulo approached. One had a rifle over the crook of his arm, the breech broken. The other one grabbed the pony's rein. It threw up its head in alarm. 'Gently,' said Paulo. 'He's had a scare.'

'Thanks,' said the gamekeeper gruffly, and tugged on the rein.

As the pony was pulled past him, Paulo noticed something odd about the deer carcass on its back. There was a plastic bag inside it and something slowly spilling out: small white beads were sticking to the pony's dark flank.

Paulo brushed them away and they stuck to his hand. When he looked at them he realized what they were: pills.

The other gamekeeper pushed Paulo out of the way and shoved the bag back into the carcass. The pony jogged, upset. Paulo recognized the man – the pale blue eyes, the acne scars and the longer scar like a cut. It was the gamekeeper who had been staring at him the previous day in the yard by the lodge. He turned to Paulo and brushed the white beads firmly off Paulo's hand, the rifle still over the crook of his arm.

'Polystyrene packing,' said the gamekeeper. 'Punters don't like to see a big bloody hole.' He wiped his hands on his trousers and snapped the rifle together. He looked as though he was checking it but the safety catch was off. Paulo was in no doubt that it was a warning to leave. He turned and walked back to the others.

Tiff's pony was munching the grass, while Li had dismounted to hold her Arab and Jess. Jess's ears pricked up as she caught sight of Paulo.

'What's up?' said Li.

'Have you got a hoof pick?' said Paulo.

Li handed him a hooked piece of metal from the pocket of her jacket.

Paulo lifted his right foot. In the tread of his boot were a couple of white dots. He eased them out with the end of the hoof pick, then scraped them carefully off the metal into his hand. Jess tried to sniff them and Paulo pushed her questing muzzle gently away.

Li watched, intrigued. 'What are those?'

'Polystyrene packing, so I'm told,' said Paulo. He got a tissue out of his pocket, carefully picked the mud off the pills, then wrapped them up and put them away. Jess sniffed at his pocket, curious. Paulo stroked her. 'Jess, they're not mints.' He took the reins back from Li and prepared to mount.

Tiff watched, wondering what on earth Li and Paulo were up to.

Paulo threw his jacket in the back of the Range Rover and climbed into the front seat beside Alex.

'Polystyrene packing?' said Alex incredulously.

Paulo did up his seat belt. He glanced in the rear-view mirror. Tiff wouldn't be able to hear. She was taking her time putting her coat in the boot. 'Yeah. This guy said they used polystyrene packing to pack the body cavity after gutting. It's so the punters don't get upset.'

'Utter rubbish,' said Alex. 'I've been hunting with my dad enough times. Anyone who's prepared to shoot an animal doesn't mind a little blood.'

Li climbed in and did up her seat belt. 'They don't mind leaving entrails on the ground outside the bothy, but they pack the carcasses with polystyrene? It doesn't add up.'

'I saw the laird out with Rob this afternoon,' said Alex. 'They had a gutted stag on the roof rack. It wasn't full of pretty polystyrene beads.'

Tiff got in, her coat dragging across the seat. Alex started the engine and switched on the wipers. They would talk about this later.

Alex pulled up in the garage beside the hostel. Tiff opened the door before he'd even cut the engine and jumped out, then ran to the front door.

Li, Paulo and Alex looked at each other. 'What's got into her?'

Li looked at her watch. 'Is it time for *EastEnders*?'

Paulo grabbed his jacket from the back seat. 'Conference – while she's occupied.'

They took their boots off and went straight to the kitchen. Delicious smells of baking wafted around them. 'Wow, Amber,' said Alex. 'What's that?'

A large roasting dish stood on a wire rack. Inside was something with a golden crust, slightly cracked to reveal a yellow spongy interior. 'Cornbread,' she replied. 'It's Roseanne's recipe; I got her to text it.'

'Wow,' said Paulo. He remembered Roseanne's cornbread well; Roseanne was Amber's housekeeper and had cooked for them when they'd all been over in New York. He leaned over the golden square and breathed in the warm fragrance. 'Mmmm,' he said.

Hex was perched on a kitchen stool. 'You wouldn't say that if you saw Amber's attempt. That's my version.'

Li looked at Hex. 'You cooked this?'

Hex shrugged. 'I just followed the instructions, that's all. No great mystery.'

'Speaking of mysteries' – Paulo threw his jacket on the stool and began to fish around in the pocket

– 'I have something rather interesting.' He lowered his voice. 'It's not poaching that's going on around here. It's drug smuggling.'

Hex and Amber looked at him incredulously. 'It's *what*?'

'We met a pair of gamekeepers,' said Paulo. 'They were transporting a dead deer on a pony and it fell over. The deer carcass split and inside was a bag full of little white pills.' He searched his inside pocket, then picked up the Range Rover keys. 'Back in a moment.' He went out and they heard the front door shut.

'Of course,' said Hex. 'That's why we found that gutted deer in the water this morning. They transport the pills in the carcass, put them in the boat, then they don't want the carcass any more. They throw them overboard.'

'I wonder what drugs they're smuggling?' said Li. 'And where they're coming from?'

Paulo came back in and began searching on the floor. 'Has anyone seen a tissue? I picked up some of those pills and they're inside it.'

For a moment they all looked around on the floor.

Paulo picked up his jacket and went through the pockets again.

'And now you can't find them?' said Alex.

'I definitely put them in my pocket.' Paulo stopped. He remembered Tiff had been in the back seat next to his jacket. 'Tiff,' he said. 'Do you think she would know what I had? Would she take them?'

'No wonder she dashed inside like a bat out of hell,' said Li.

Amber rolled her eyes. 'Oh brother.'

Alex stood up. 'If she has, she'd better not be alone. If it's like the stuff I had it's horrible.'

He went out into the corridor. The sound of the TV floated towards him – the news on high volume.

At the far end, the TV room door opened. Tiff twirled into the corridor, and skipped lightly towards the crowd coming to join her.

Alex caught her in his arms. He'd expected her to struggle and maybe even kick him but instead she swayed to and fro. She was trying to get him to dance. He looked into her face. Her expression was cherubic – completely unlike the sour Tiff they knew. Her eyes were flicking quickly from side to side. She had definitely taken something.

She slithered past him and ran into Paulo. 'Got any music, cowboy? Do you dance?' She twirled in front of him, round and round, delighted by the movement.

Paulo gave Alex a long-suffering look and pushed her back into the TV room. She went easily, but he didn't follow her in. He slammed the door as though he'd trapped a rat in there.

'Should we call a doctor?' asked Li.

Alex shook his head. 'She seems OK. She's not like I was; she's having a good time.'

'How long does it last?'

Alex shrugged. 'Who knows? We don't know what it was.'

The TV sound jumped. Tiff was channel-hopping.

'We'd better not leave her alone,' said Amber. 'She might not stay in there. We'll watch her in shifts.'

'I'll do the first,' sighed Hex. 'After all, I've done it before.'

There was silence. Tiff had turned off the TV. 'Uh-oh,' said Amber. 'The pacifier isn't working.'

Hex put his hand on the door. His face was grim. 'Check on me in half an hour.'

Paulo said, 'Let's have a look in the Range Rover. I had two pills; one of them might still be in there.'

Li, Amber and Alex joined Paulo outside. Paulo had scoured the entire Range Rover twice.

'Nothing?' said Alex.

Paulo shook his head.

'It's not in her room,' said Li.

'And it's not in her pockets,' said Amber. 'She must have taken them both.'

Paulo straightened up and ran a hand through his hair. 'That was good evidence. We could have taken that to the police. I shouldn't have let them out of my sight.'

Li spluttered, 'None of us thought she'd actually go through your pockets.'

'We can still go to the police,' said Amber. 'A pick-up by boat, a slick method of transportation across the moors – all the suspicious stuff you guys saw at night . . . It's a big operation, transporting big quantities. There must be a factory close by.'

'Paulo and Li, you've seen the strongest evidence,' said Alex. 'You come with me.'

Li turned to Amber. 'Amber, will you be all right here to take over from Hex?'

Amber sighed. 'It'll be an experience, I suppose.'

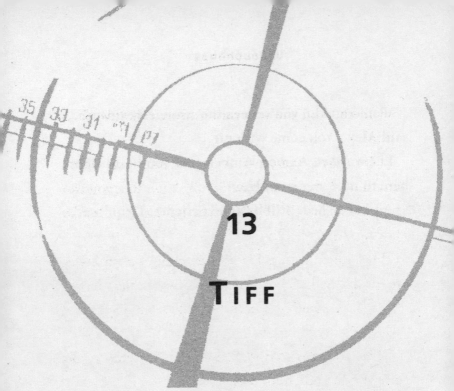

13

TIFF

Tiff was sitting quietly on the floor in the TV room. Hex had done his best to keep the atmosphere calming – the TV was off, the curtains were closed because the sun wouldn't be going down yet. At first she'd been leaping around like a monkey, excited by every sound, trying to get him into the same mood. Now she was sitting with her back to the cold radiator, looking thoroughly bored, her knees pulled up to her chest. Aside from that she looked fairly normal, except that her pupils were huge black holes and she kept grinding her teeth. And she was rather more talkative than usual.

'You guys, you just want to stop me doing anything. I should be having fun. You think you can brainwash me to be like other people . . . It's so boring.'

Hex tuned it out. He was catching up on his e-mails. He had friends in online communities all over the world, some of whom he hadn't e-mailed for a while. Plenty to be getting on with.

'Everything is so dull,' said Tiff. 'Everything and everybody. Dull, dull, dull.'

Hex was looking at the screen but no longer paying attention to it. He was listening to Tiff in spite of himself. He was thinking about what it was like before he met the others. Bored rigid by school, he was an outsider no one understood. Everything seemed trivial and unchallenging. Then he'd discovered the Internet and had reinvented himself in a virtual world. He had friends – people he'd met online who were interested in the same things. He was e-mailing some of them now. He didn't know what most of them looked like, how old they were, what their real names were – in the online universe, you chose your own name, you were a person you'd invented.

'You won't understand,' said Tiff. 'Nobody does.' She ground her teeth again.

Perhaps he should tell Tiff to go online. Sort her life out that way. His online world had been more real than reality. He'd quite happily have become a pixel, slid into a machine and stayed in virtual reality for eternity. That was until he'd met Amber, Alex, Paulo and Li. Virtual Hex had thought he knew what excitement and danger were. If he made a wrong move on the Internet his machine could be trashed – his virtual world could end. It seemed like high stakes indeed. Now, though, he could pay for mistakes with real injuries, his actual life. Not only that; other people could be hurt, crippled or killed. His four friends, to whom he was closer than he had ever been to anyone, were still alive today because of things he had done. He was alive because of things they had done. Together they'd saved people, brought killers to justice, changed people's lives. They'd done things that mattered, and that made the real world worth living in.

He looked at the e-mail windows he had open, the friends waiting for a reply. The first was to ScaryHarry. He'd 'known' ScaryHarry for years. He was a reformed hacker who designed security systems for banks. Not the kind of security systems that dealt with hold-ups; the kind that kept out other hackers like him. Hex didn't quite feel able to relate to ScaryHarry right now. He miniaturized the window. Next was johnsmith. Hex knew even less about johnsmith – all lower case – than he did about ScaryHarry. Hex was intrigued by him – johnsmith revelled in enigmatic e-mail exchanges yet had chosen the world's most deliberately anonymous name. But that would have to wait until later too.

He glanced at the clock in the bottom right-hand corner of the screen. Any moment, Amber would take over.

'Dull,' said Tiff again. She fidgeted in the pockets of her denim jacket and pulled out a dark tube. She looked at it and shook it, inspecting it minutely. It was her green glow stick from the morning. 'It's dead,' she said. 'What a pity.' She flicked it from side to side, trying to start it again.

She looked so genuinely sad. It was such an unexpected sight, after her habitual carping sarcasm that Hex found himself looking at the dark stick too. It reminded him of cramped places, of breathing in dust, of a dead body. 'Sometimes,' he said, 'you think you're going to die and you don't. That stops you thinking life is dull.'

It came out before he even thought it. He buried his head in his hands. What was he doing?

'Wow,' said Tiff. 'That is so profound.'

She was stoned out of her head, thought Hex. Tomorrow she wouldn't remember a word he'd said. He looked at his watch. 'You need to have a good talk to Amber,' he said confidently. 'She'll understand exactly where you're coming from.'

The door opened. Right on cue, Amber was here.

Hex was on his feet immediately. 'See you in a bit,' he said, and closed the door behind him.

Tiff was talking immediately. 'I've misjudged Hex. He's a really good listener. He's so cool. Really deep. No one's ever listened to me like that before.'

Amber was wary. Tiff laid back, thoughtful? What on earth was that drug she'd taken? Perhaps they were wrong to go to the police if it could tame a hellcat like Tiff.

'Hex says I need to have a talk to you, woman to woman,' said Tiff.

Thanks, Hex, thought Amber.

'OK,' said the officer, scanning the statement. Alex, Paulo and Li sat on the opposite side of the table from him. 'You have speculated that there might be a drugs factory somewhere on the estate, that drugs are being made and smuggled out inside freshly killed deer. Do you have any thoughts on where the factory might be?'

They shook their heads.

'You saw these gamekeepers with carcasses full of small white objects. When you asked the gamekeepers what they were they said they were bits of polystyrene packing material. Is that right?'

Paulo realized how lame the story sounded. They'd decided not to mention that Tiff had taken the pills. There was no proof that that was where she'd got them. Without the evidence, there was nothing to it. 'Yes,' said Paulo.

'I've been on shoots before,' said Alex. 'No one packs carcasses with polystyrene to make them look pretty.'

The officer shrugged. 'It's a top-flight luxury establishment. I've had tea up there and they put a doily between the cup and the saucer.' He continued to read from the statement. 'You think there is smuggling going on. You saw two gamekeepers, who you cannot identify, loading carcasses into a boat off the Kyle of Tongue. Then you saw a carcass washed up in a cave on Rowan Island.'

'That's right,' said Li. She looked at Paulo. This wasn't going well.

'It doesn't sound like much, does it?' said Alex.

The officer looked at the statement. 'On the face of it, no. But we'd always rather people came to us with suspicions of any sort – it's our job to find out whether they're founded on fact or not. We'll send an officer up to talk to the laird. From what you've said, there might be a bit of minor poaching going on. But I doubt there's any drug running. We will of course ask to see the packing material but I doubt it's anything to worry about. The laird's a prominent figure in the community – he just funded a new computer wing for the local school. Minor members of royalty come on his shoots. I very much doubt he's up to anything.' He turned the statement round and indicated a space at the bottom with his pen. 'If you'd just like to read it and sign here.'

Hex looked up as Paulo, Alex and Li came into the kitchen.

'Hex, have you found anything?' asked Alex. He pulled out a chair at the wooden table and sat down opposite him.

As soon as they left the police station Alex had texted Hex and asked him to find whatever information he could about Frank Allen, the laird.

'Well,' said Hex, 'our laird is more barrow boy than Barrow-in-Furness.'

'What do you mean?' said Li.

'He's not Scottish. He's from the East End of London and he inherited a lot of money from his father a few years ago, which seems to be when he started the lodge. A number of the Sunday papers have done profiles of him. Before he arrived,

Glaickvullin village was tiny, like Tongue. He moved in and did up the castle. First builders came, then farmhands and mechanics. Then, once it was up and running, it was chefs, waitresses, gamekeepers, cleaners, bookkeepers. New shops opened. The local school reopened and he built a computer wing. They were about to close the doctor's surgery as there weren't enough people in the village to make it worthwhile. Now there's a mini hospital there. He's practically reinvented Glaickvullin.'

Paulo sat down at the table and put his head in his hands. 'No wonder the police don't believe us. He's the local patron saint. Alex, you saw him. What was he like?'

Alex shrugged. 'Not really a country person. Didn't fit. But that's about all I noticed.'

'I wonder where he got all his money?' said Li. 'Does it say?'

'Property, it seems,' replied Hex, typing.

Paulo checked his watch and got up. 'Time for someone to relieve Amber. How's the patient?'

'Talkative,' said Hex. 'You'll see.'

Paulo went out and closed the door.

'We need evidence,' said Li. 'How do we get that?'

Alex spoke quietly. 'There are two places where we've seen strange things, the bothy and the moor. We go and do some surveillance. We take the camera. Those guys must be leaving some evidence of what they are really up to, and we're going to find it. Hex, can you find out any more about our laird and his employees?'

'Just on that now,' smiled Hex. He hit SEND. Finally he'd found something he wanted to e-mail ScaryHarry about.

'Our guys operate at night,' said Li. 'We could go out after supper.'

Amber came back into the room and clapped Hex on the back. 'You've made a real friend there, honey.'

Hex looked round in horror. 'Have I?'

'Oh yes,' said Amber. She looked at Li and Alex. 'What's the score?'

14

SURVEILLANCE

Hex showed Li the grid reference on his GPS. 'Here's where you saw the six-wheelers.'

Li nodded.

It was dark. There was no moon. A chilly wind blew across the open moor. Ever since the rain it had been a lot colder. They were glad of their black fleeces and balaclavas. They had smeared camouflage cream on their faces, necks and wrists so that they could blend seamlessly into the landscape.

Li swept her torch around the area. 'Where are we going to lay up?'

Hex's torch found a wiggly trench in the ground. A dry stream bed. 'Perfect,' he said, and vaulted in.

He vaulted straight back out.

'What's wrong?'

'It's full of freezing water,' he groaned. 'I'd forgotten about all that rain.'

Li jumped in. The water lapped over her boots. She knelt down and shuddered. 'Let's hope we don't have to wait for long.'

Hex slipped in again, grumbled and ducked down. It was unpleasant but it was good cover. They could see in all directions and if headlights came along they could stay out of sight.

Li shook herself, trying to get warm. 'Of course, they may not come here again.'

'They'd better come,' shivered Hex.

A light burned in the window of the bothy down below, so that it looked like a tiny lantern. Amber and Alex lay on their stomachs watching it, camouflaged like Li and Hex.

Amber was checking the map. 'Is that it?' There was always a chance they'd got the wrong bothy in the dark.

Alex checked the grid reference. 'Yes, that's the one.'

The two friends switched their torches off. They crept down the hill carefully, working by feel. In the light from the window they could see the six-wheeled ATV – and another vehicle, a normal quad. Did the gamekeepers have guests? In the window they could see three figures. It seemed they did.

Alex stopped and sat down. He took the video camera out of his pack and began filming. 'This is the perfect hideaway,' he whispered. 'Miles from any roads. No one's going to stumble across it in the night by accident.'

'Except if they're in a drug-induced haze.'

Alex knew she was joking but he still couldn't get the experience out of his mind. 'It wasn't a haze,' he said. 'It was like being possessed.'

'Do you think Tiff's taken the same thing?'

'No,' muttered Alex. 'She's enjoying it. There's no way you could enjoy what I had.'

The men were still just standing in the room,

talking. 'Come on,' growled Alex softly. 'Stop discussing the football and do something weird, like you did the other night.'

A chink of light appeared about a metre to the left of the window. The door was opening. A figure came out, silhouetted against the golden lamplight. He was tall, heavily built.

'Ah,' muttered Alex. 'We haven't seen you before. Smile for the camera.'

One of the gamekeepers came out, carrying something large and heavy in his arms. Amber squeezed Alex's arm. It was a deer carcass.

The other man came out with another deer carcass. They loaded them onto the six-wheeler. The big man got on the quad and started it. The headlights winked on. Instinctively Amber and Alex ducked, but they were well hidden. One of the gamekeepers went to lock the door, then climbed on the ATV behind the other. The two bikes revved and roared away.

'Is that it?' said Amber.

Alex lowered the camera and switched it off. 'We should have given the camera to Hex and Li.'

* * *

'I wonder how Paulo's getting on with Tiff,' said Li.

'I hope he's braced for some deep, meaningful conversations,' said Hex. 'That drug's made her very introspective.'

The sound of a lone vehicle drifted across the night sky. Immediately they focused on the job. The sound came closer and a waft of exhaust fumes drifted over to them. Li spotted a cluster of headlights, bouncing through the sky.

'Two vehicles,' she whispered. 'There was only one before. They've brought a friend.'

The two friends ducked well down in the stream bed. Now they would see what really went on here.

They heard the bikes pull up and the engines stop, but they kept down as low as possible. Their heads were only metres away from the wheels.

The six-wheeler's lights were still on. One of the gamekeepers walked a short way away from it, shining a torch on the ground. The other unclipped some elastic ropes securing the carcasses.

The other bike, a normal quad, had a lone rider. He stood up, silhouetted against the six-wheeler's lights. He was big, very powerfully built, well over six feet tall. Even in silhouette they could see he was dressed differently from the gamekeepers. He wore baggy jeans and a hoodie pulled up so that he looked like he was wearing a shroud. He was powerfully built and the baggy clothes made him look even bigger. City clothes, thought Hex. Not country gear.

When the big man talked, the other two stopped what they were doing and listened attentively. That could only mean one thing.

Li whispered to Hex, 'Those gamekeepers are really scared of this guy.'

One of them put the torch in his mouth, ghoulishly reddening his face. He knelt down and there was a metallic noise; then his face was obscured by a shadow. The big man waited, his face dark under the hood. What were they doing?

The kneeling gamekeeper pulled something out of the ground and went behind it. Down behind it. Li and Hex heard a sound like feet on metal rungs.

A few moments later there was another sound like an engine starting.

Li gripped Hex's arm. It was the sound she had heard in the cave.

A light flooded into the sky from deep in the ground, as though someone had turned a spotlight on. It illuminated the cloud above – and the big square trapdoor that the man had opened in the ground. So that's where he had disappeared.

Li and Hex held their breath. Something was buried under the heather.

They heard feet on rungs again. The second gamekeeper was waiting with one of the deer carcasses. Arms reached out from behind the trapdoor and dug into the carcass. Li and Hex caught a glimpse of something blue, bright royal blue, being pulled out of the split where the carcass had been gutted. A small blue drum, about the size of a rugby ball.

The gamekeeper descended out of sight and the big man followed him down. The other gamekeeper dumped the remaining carcass beside the trapdoor, climbed down a few rungs, eased another blue drum out of the carcass, then disappeared.

The light shone into the night sky. It seemed to beckon: *Come closer. Come and look.* It seemed wrong to just sit there.

The two friends heard footsteps coming up the ladder again. The trapdoor was pulled down sharply, extinguishing the light.

Li let out her breath very slowly. 'That sound was what I heard in the cave. It's a generator.'

Hex spoke rapidly, excitedly. 'That's the missing link. That's their factory. And who's that big guy?'

'Should we report back? Or should we stay?'

'I think we'd better stay,' said Hex.

Tiff was lying on the sofa, huddled in a purple blanket. A reading lamp threw a soft pool of light over her blonde hair. Paulo was sitting against the radiator, still watching her.

'I'm sorry,' said Tiff.

The pattern had been the same for the past few hours. She would look like she was going to sleep, then would suddenly start talking, nattering about whatever popped into her butterfly brain.

Paulo wished he felt as wide awake as she did. 'Sorry for what?'

'I stole your stash,' said Tiff.

'My what?' said Paulo.

'Your stash. I've seen E before. I know what it looks like.'

Paulo sighed. 'I don't take drugs,' he said. 'And you shouldn't either.'

'What were you doing with that stuff then?' said Tiff. 'I found it in your pocket.'

How much should he tell her? She might say the wrong thing somewhere and ruin their cover. 'I was going to take them to the police,' he explained. At least that was the truth.

The front door banged and then Alex and Amber walked in.

'Are you guys still here?' said Amber. 'I'd have thought you'd be tired by now.'

Paulo yawned forcefully. 'One of us is.'

'Where have you been?' asked Tiff.

'Night orienteering,' said Alex. 'You wouldn't have liked it.'

Tiff checked who had come back. 'Where's Hex? I'm not going to sleep before he gets back.'

'He's coming,' said Amber. 'They went a different way. Paulo, I'll take over if you want.'

Paulo got up and stumbled out. 'Goodnight all.'

Amber settled down on the beanbag next to the radiator. She waved at Alex as he went out.

Tiff looked at Amber somewhat balefully, then put her head down on a cushion, as if trying to get comfortable. The gesture said, *I'm not going to talk to you.* Fine, thought Amber. I don't want to talk to you either. In fact maybe she'd get some sleep.

But Tiff started talking again. Her voice was quiet, the hostility gone. 'My mum married again,' she told Amber. 'She doesn't want a kid around. She can't wait to get away on her own with my stepfather.' There was none of the usual sarcasm in her voice. Not even bitterness. Just sadness.

'I'm nothing more than a babysitting problem,' she went on. 'I have to be farmed out, sent on trips and kept occupied. Brainwashed so that I don't want anything. They want a robot, not a daughter. They've no idea who I am. I don't matter.'

Her words stirred powerful memories. Once upon a time Amber had thought the same about her parents. They'd left her behind while they went abroad. She later discovered that they were away on missions, but at the time Amber had thought they didn't want to be bothered with her. 'I know how you feel,' she said quietly.

Tiff shifted and something rolled out of the covers onto the floor. It looked like a fat pen. Amber reached forward to retrieve it but Tiff snatched it back and looked at it thoughtfully. It was a spent glow stick, but Tiff was looking at it as if it was fascinating.

'That's a dead one, Tiff,' said Amber. 'It's not going to come back on.'

Tiff fixed her with a steely look. 'It's a symbol.' She gazed at it and her voice became sad again. 'There are dark places you would never understand. Hex understands, though. He understands what it's like to die.'

Oh dear, thought Amber. We've been through the sensitive phase. Now she's getting morbid. And just when I thought I'd get some sleep.

15

TRAPDOOR

Li made almost no noise as she crawled along the ground towards the faint glow of light leaking around the edge of the trapdoor. She was cold and wet but she kept her movements very slow, as though she was stalking it. They had no idea how thick or thin the ground around it was and whether the men below could hear people moving on the surface.

Hex watched her tracer on his palmtop screen. They were going to mark the exact position of the trapdoor so that they could find it later. Since they'd missed it in broad daylight, it was obviously well hidden.

Not far now. Li wondered what was below her hands and feet and this seemingly solid piece of moor. Was it another cave? Or some kind of manmade structure? How big was it?

Her heart thudded as she moved her hands and knees gently towards the square of light. It glinted off a pair of open eyes. She froze, horrified, then realized it was one of the dead deer. She started to move again.

The trapdoor trembled and she heard a metallic scraping. Footsteps, ringing below her hands and knees. Someone was coming up. She'd have to abort.

If she shouted to Hex she'd be heard. She rolled to the side, twisting so that she got as far away from the opening and the bikes as possible. The trapdoor opened, throwing a glow into the sky. She lay still, trying to calm her breathing. Had she gone far enough away? Had Hex got out of sight?

One of the gamekeepers came out, followed by the big man. Both wore pale surgical masks and white papery overalls over their clothes, like radiation suits. They walked towards her, the gamekeeper flashing his torch along the ground. They were coming straight for her.

She rolled again and felt the ground disappear. She was on the edge of the stream bed. She'd have to stay here – if she went in they'd hear the splash. She tried to flatten herself into the grass. The big man's overalls were enormous to fit over his baggy clothes. The gamekeeper looked puny by comparison.

They stopped. Li was less than a metre away from them. She stayed stock-still, hardly daring to breathe.

The big man pulled off his mask and ripped open his suit. He bent over as he stepped out of it and Li saw a flash of his face in the torchlight. His features looked Eastern European and distorted, like a boxer who carried many old injuries. The hooked nose was spread, the eyes were slits; the whole face was dotted with piercings – diamonds winked in his nose, his bottom lip, his cheek. As he straightened up, his face slipped into the shadows of his hood. Only the pinpoints of light from the diamonds remained visible, as though he had tiny eyes in the wrong places.

The other man had pulled his mask down around his chin. He put a cigarette between his lips and brought out a lighter. The flame illuminated dark brows, frowning eyes concentrating on the cigarette he was lighting.

Li kept watching. The cigarette caught, his face relaxed and he put the lighter out. But she'd got a good look at his face. She'd be able to identify him.

He put the lighter back in his pocket and took a long, satisfying drag. A strange, chemical smell came off the papery trousers. It reminded Li of the chemistry labs at school.

The big man passed his overalls and mask back to the smaller man. 'I don't want any of those green pills,' he said. His voice was quiet, but dangerous. 'What were they?'

'E and ketamine,' said the gamekeeper.

'Yeah, well they're rubbish,' said the big man. 'People take them, they get a bad trip, they don't come back to my dealers. I've got important clients who don't want their heads messed with. You give me just pure Ebenezer, you got it?'

Ebenezer. E. A name for ecstasy.

The gamekeeper nodded.

'You got the capacity? I can go anywhere and get

rubbish. You give me good product, OK? I don't want to find you've put rubbish in there because you don't have time.'

'We can do it,' said the gamekeeper. 'We'll be ready for you tomorrow night. Just name a time.'

'You better be ready, brother. You've got my money. I don't like being short-changed.' The man looked the gamekeeper up and down. 'If the guys could see you now – dressed like Lord Sprockett.'

Hex was crouching behind the bikes. He saw the man turn away from the gamekeeper and start walking towards him, the torch swinging in his hand.

Hex's blood pressure hit the roof. Which vehicle had the big man come on? The quad or the six-wheeler? The quad, wasn't it?

Hex watched the swing of the man's arms. On the downswing of the torch he rolled swiftly behind the six-wheel ATV.

The big man got on the quad. The engine roared into life; next would be the headlights. Hex flattened himself on the ground as the big man opened the throttle. The wheels passed within a metre of his hands.

That just left the other man. And where was Li?

Hex peered up cautiously. The side of the gamekeeper's face was gently illuminated by the light from the open hatch. The end of the cigarette glowed like a coal as the gamekeeper drew in a breath. Smoke curled over the red tip. Well, at least that cigarette made him easy to spot. Hex couldn't see Li at all, but now the other man had gone, there was nothing to distract the gamekeeper from any tiny noise that she might make. How long did it take to smoke a cigarette? Three minutes? Five minutes? Stay hidden, Li, prayed Hex.

The gamekeeper inhaled – and stopped. The red tip paused in the air; he held his breath and listened.

Li felt a trickle of sweat pouring down her back. He had seen her.

'Hello?' he said. His voice was rough, Glaswegian.

Li saw him peer into the gloom at her.

Then there was a faint patter of feet on metal; a rustle in the heather. Some nocturnal creature had been exploring the ATV. The gamekeeper walked over to the bike to investigate. Li breathed out a long, careful sigh.

Hex rolled into the heather and lay still. The gamekeeper flashed his torch over the bike, took a last drag on his cigarette, then dropped it. Its red glow disappeared under the toe of his boot. He pulled his mask back on, walked back to the trapdoor, climbed in and pulled it shut.

Li stood up and jogged on the spot, trying to warm up. She was freezing. She could see Hex's pale blue palmtop light like a will-o'-the-wisp. She ran gratefully over to him.

'Phew – that was close. Did you get the position of the trapdoor?'

Hex nodded. 'Roughly. We'll have to come back and look in daylight. It's too dangerous to do more now.'

They jogged away, prepared to duck down again at any moment, but the trapdoor stayed closed. It was a relief to move after holding still for so long.

Li slowed to a walk. She felt mentally exhausted. 'I really thought that guy with the cigarette had seen me. Thank heavens for small nocturnal animals.'

'Or large ones,' said Hex. His eyes were twinkling in the torchlight. Li looked at him, puzzled, and he ran his fingers lightly up her arm like a scampering animal.

'It was you!' She rubbed him on the arm. 'You probably saved my bacon.'

Li shuddered. 'They're making a big pick-up sometime tomorrow night, but we don't know when.' Her hands were around a steaming mug of hot chocolate, but lying still for so long in wet clothes had chilled her to the bone.

She and Hex were in the kitchen, giving the others a resumé of what they had seen on the moor. Tiff had finally drifted into a deep sleep and Amber felt it was safe to leave her.

Paulo stared into his mug of hot chocolate – Amber had just got him and Alex out of their beds. 'That's got to be the factory,' said Paulo. He looked sleepy but his brain had grasped the facts swiftly.

'Is that enough to go to the police with?' said Amber.

'I think we need more,' said Alex. 'We could tell the police to ambush them, but they might only get the gamekeepers.'

Hex nodded. 'We've got to get a good look at the factory during the day when they're not around, find the trapdoor. If we can't find it, the police won't.'

Amber sighed. 'If only we'd given you and Li the video camera, you could have filmed what you saw and that would be enough.'

'There's more than just the factory,' said Hex. 'There's a big deal going through. If we could find out when they're making the handover, we could get the hooded guy too.'

Li nodded. 'He's not just a dealer, he's a mega-dealer. He was talking about major clients, a string of dealers. He's big time. If the gamekeepers get busted too early, he'll just walk away.'

Paulo yawned. 'If we're going to do something, we'd better move fast. The police will probably question the gamekeepers sometime later today about the "polystyrene". That will put them on alert.'

'There's no point trying to get more evidence now,' said Hex. 'They're busy at night. We'll just run into them again. We're better off leaving it until the morning.'

Amber sat back thoughtfully. 'OK, we have two objectives: to find physical evidence of the factory; and to find out when the deal's being done.'

'Three objectives,' yawned Paulo. 'Get some sleep.'

'Four,' said Alex. His voice was serious. 'Stay alive. My dad's mate was on a mission watching the IRA when he stumbled across a drugs factory in someone's back room. The next day three guys came and cut his head off with a chainsaw.' He looked at his four friends earnestly. 'We've stayed undercover until now. Let's keep it that way.'

16

RACE AGAINST TIME

At 7 a.m. Li opened her curtains. Four hours' sleep wasn't really enough. The sun was already starting to evaporate the dew into a light mist. It was a captivating sight — it almost made her glad to be up.

Someone pounded on the door.

'Yeah, it's OK,' she called. 'I'm up.'

Paulo's voice answered her. 'Tiff's gone again.'

She threw on some clothes and pounded down the stairs.

In the hall Alex was already making plans. 'Li, you

search the attics, Amber the bedrooms, Paulo the ground floor. Hex and I will take the outbuildings.'

Amber, a slice of bread in one hand, spoke between mouthfuls. She was a diabetic and had to make sure she ate regularly. 'Hex, couldn't you just look her up on your thingy?'

'I've done all that,' said Hex. 'I couldn't see her so I tried calling her. Her phone's in her room.'

Amber gulped down the rest of her breakfast as she climbed the stairs.

Amber had found nothing. She strode out of the front door. Li and Paulo were standing in the drive.

'Anything?'

They shook their heads.

The mist was lifting, making the valley glow. From the garage came the clunk of the Range Rover door, then Hex and Alex came out.

Alex saw the group and shook his head. 'Zilch. She's vanished into thin air.'

'Most of her stuff's still in her bedroom,' said Amber, 'so she hasn't gone to the airport or anything. But her walking boots have gone.'

'Typical,' sighed Hex. 'The only way that lazy trout would go for a walk is to annoy us.'

'All the safety equipment's still here,' said Alex. 'Ropes, helmets, etc.'

'Pur-leeze!' exclaimed Li. 'She's not going to go for an energetic climb.'

'I looked at her alarm clock in case she'd set it to go out early,' said Amber. 'No clues there. It wasn't even on.'

Alex looked up into the hills. A gentle breeze made the heather ripple. 'We'd better find her before she blunders into something she shouldn't.'

The Ordnance Survey map was spread out on the kitchen table.

'She can't have got far,' said Paulo. 'She's not very fit.'

'But we don't know what time she left,' said Li. 'We went to bed at three; she could have been gone for hours.'

Amber looked at the map. 'She hates hill walking. So she won't have gone up here.' She pointed to the contour lines that indicated the steep hill that rose at the back of the hostel.

'Most likely she went along the road,' said Hex.

Alex looked at the map, mentally dividing it up. He had learned a number of ways of searching for a lost person. You covered the area according to a set pattern, which meant you didn't miss anywhere. 'I think we should take two quad bikes; the rest of us can go in the Range Rover and search the roads.'

'I'll take a quad,' said Paulo.

'Me too,' said Amber. She looked at Hex. 'You coming?'

Hex snorted. 'Not if you're driving.'

'Actually, Hex,' said Alex, 'you'd better come in the Range Rover. You can monitor everyone on tracers. And we'd better have just one person on each quad so we've got something to bring her back on.'

'Wish we'd thought to put a tracer on *her*,' muttered Li.

Paulo was looking at the map. 'There are a few farm buildings in the area. We might get lucky with some of those.'

'We just have to hope she didn't hitch a ride somewhere,' said Amber.

'I don't think she'd leave her luggage,' said Li.

Alex stood up. It was time to go. 'OK, guys, keep in contact, usual protocols. If you have to go into a mobile blind spot, tell someone first so we know where you are. Let's get her back before she gets herself killed.'

Scottish farmyards were so different from Argentinian ones, thought Paulo. His parents' ranch was full of wide open spaces. This farm in Scotland was overlooked by brooding hills, as though somebody had taken a regular ranch and rumpled it up to fit into a much smaller space. On an Argentinian ranch everything was wooden – the fences, the buildings, the arch over the entrance. In Scotland the buildings had evolved out of a motley collection of scavenged materials – a stone croft with a patched roof, a big barn made of breeze blocks and corrugated iron. And then there was the mud. Apart from the rain the day before, it had been dry most of the time they had been in Scotland. So why were all the farmyards he'd seen wet and muddy?

A man in grimy blue overalls was pouring diesel

into his tractor. Paulo parked the bike and walked up to him. He asked the question he had asked at many farmyards already.

'I'm looking for a missing girl – five foot two, blonde hair. Have you seen anyone around the place?'

The man sucked in his bottom lip as though giving the question careful consideration. 'No. But you're welcome to look around for yourself.'

Paulo walked off towards the breeze-block hay barn.

Amber had gone in the opposite direction, across the moor. She took it slowly, looking from left to right across the wide open space. Already there were people about – early morning walkers mostly. She passed a burned area of heather, the branches twisted like black coral. The sound of a shot rang across the moor. Amber stopped and listened for the body falling but she must have been too far away to hear it. That was a hazard she hadn't thought of. There were people out here shooting. What if the silly girl had wandered into the path of a bullet?

To Amber's left the ground sloped away steeply. It made a sort of crescent shape, and down in the bowl was a small square ruined barn. Better check it. How much longer was it going to take to find her? Already it was ten o'clock. The morning was ticking away and they had work to do.

Amber turned the handlebars towards the slope. The bike began to run away with her. She braked hard. It was steeper than she thought. She turned away instead: overturning an ATV wasn't smart. They were heavy and could break your neck. She sighed. More delays. She looked for another way round.

Alex met Li and Hex back at the Range Rover. They were at the top of the main street of Tongue and had searched the village without success. They climbed into the vehicle wearily.

Li buckled her seat belt. 'We could try Glaickvullin.'

Alex started the engine and moved out into the traffic. 'I suppose so. But it would take her ages to walk there – a good few hours. We might just have to report her to the police.'

'Don't they have to be missing for longer than a few hours?' asked Hex.

On the dashboard Alex's phone rang. Li looked at the display. 'It's a text from Paulo.' She brought up the message, then glanced at Alex. '*Am stalking a rare bird with pink plumage. Will try to bring her out without scaring her.*'

Paulo was in another farm, in another barn. This at least smelled like home, a clean, heady smell, almost spicy. Newly made hay had been baled and stacked like a wall of giant building blocks. A steel ladder led to the top, nearly six metres up.

Paulo heard the movement again, like a rustle. He put his phone away and pattered up the ladder to the top.

A big pair of eyes looked back at him. He'd seen her from the ground: the fluorescent pink flashes on her Punkyfish leggings were a dead giveaway. Tiff looked forlorn, her eyes surrounded by dark shadows, hay falling out of her pale hair, her ponytail dishevelled.

Paulo took his time, as he had with the frightened

pony. Tiff might still decide to run away. He sat down beside her. 'How's it going?'

Tiff sat up, pulling her knees into her chest. She looked at her feet. Paulo got the feeling it was easier than looking at him. Was she embarrassed?

'You feeling a bit rough?' said Paulo.

'I needed to think,' she said to her Puma sneakers. 'Now you can take me back.'

She was embarrassed, thought Paulo, but she's covering it up. He climbed down the ladder and held it for her. At least they'd found her safe and sound.

Alex and the others were locking up the Range Rover as Paulo bumped down off the hillside onto the drive. As soon as he braked, Tiff climbed off.

'You can all go to hell.' She stalked into the hostel and slammed the front door.

Li looked at Paulo. 'You must have had a pleasant journey.'

Alex let out his breath in a long hiss. 'We've wasted several hours running around after her when we could have been doing other things. Are there any volunteers for nanny duty?'

Paulo cut the engine. 'I'll take her for a walk to clear her head. She wasn't too bad on the way back.'

Alex nodded. 'Let's make plans. Conference in the kitchen in ten minutes?'

In his room Hex set his palmtop recharging. It had been used a lot and he wanted to top up the batteries. Across the landing he could hear Tiff as she made a phone call in her room; he couldn't distinguish actual words, but the complaining tone was clear. No doubt she was filling in some friend on the injustices of the morning. He went back out onto the landing just as Tiff came out of her room. She was wearing a purple hoodie and dragging her suitcase along the corridor. She saw him and straightened up.

'I'm going. I'm too stressed. I've been telling my parents the things you've made me do and they've just told me they've booked me into a health spa. They've sent you a fax to confirm.'

Hex could hardly believe the troublemaking little minx had done anything so convenient. 'You're going right now?'

'My parents' PA is coming for me in a taxi. There's nothing you can do to stop me.'

Hex was tempted to beg her to stay for one last day of overwhelming fun. Instead he picked up her case. 'Better get this downstairs.' Tiff followed him down.

Outside in the drive he heard the crunch of tyres on the gravel and saw Paulo looking through the spy hole in the front door.

'It's a taxi,' said Paulo, and straightened up. The others relaxed visibly. Hex realized they must have been on the alert for trouble.

Tiff saw her audience. 'I'm going,' she said dramatically, 'and there's nothing you can do.'

Amber came out of the office. In her hands was a fax, which she read and then passed to Alex. Alex skimmed over the text and handed it to Paulo before opening the door. A woman in a cream-coloured suit was stepping out of the taxi and looking expectantly at the hostel.

'Before we hand you over, I'll just go and make sure this lady checks out,' said Alex to Tiff. He strode across the drive, his hand outstretched in greeting.

Tiff watched him balefully. 'You won't take my word for anything, will you?'

Amber met Paulo's eye. He gave her a long-suffering look.

Alex came back. 'Yep. She checks out. Going somewhere nice, Tiff?'

Tiff took her case from Hex. 'Nicer than this dump. Somewhere you creeps could never afford.'

She walked awkwardly out to the waiting taxi, her suitcase dragging a wake through the gravel.

Alex came back in and shut the door. His face broke out in a big grin and he punched his fist into the air in triumph. 'Yes! Let's get going.'

17

SECRETS

'All clear,' said Paulo.

Alex dropped to one knee in front of the door to the bothy and slipped a probe into the keyhole. He let his eyes zone out as he felt his way, gently flipping the tumblers of the lock.

It was stiff; it wasn't coming as easily as he'd hoped. Alex could feel himself getting frustrated. He took a deep breath and slowed down. You couldn't rush something like this. Think calm, he said to himself, and feel your way. You never know when it's going to go.

He felt the satisfying click as the bolt inside the lock pulled back. He turned the handle and the door swung open.

Paulo dived in after Alex and closed the door. Inside, the bothy was like a small, sparsely furnished cottage, the kind you saw reconstructed in museums. A fireplace was dusted with ash. An oil lamp stood on the simple wooden table. Two rough benches stood by the fire. A washing line stretched across the room for drying wet clothes.

'So what secrets is this place keeping?' said Paulo.

'Secrets that have to be locked away,' said Alex. 'Search everything.'

Paulo started with the fireplace. There was a pile of wood to the left-hand side. He lifted a few pieces.

The middle was hollow. There was something inside, wrapped in a blue plastic bag. Paulo pulled it out and unwrapped the plastic. Inside were lots of small Ziploc bags; hundreds of them, each about ten centimetres long. 'Alex?'

Alex looked up from the narrow bunk at the other end of the room. 'Interesting but not incriminating.'

Paulo peered into the hole again. 'There's another

lot.' He pulled out a green plastic bag. Inside were more Ziploc bags, this time yellow. 'Hmm. Two colours of bag. Two products?'

'Probably,' said Alex.

Paulo rewrapped the bags and put them back. He moved on to the fireplace and poked the ashy remains with some tongs. It didn't look like it was all wood ash. There were charred scraps of cardboard – cardboard that had been cut into small pieces. He swished away the ash at the back. Here was something. A few small lumps of royal blue plastic, as if something had melted.

'Alex – they've been burning cardboard here. And something else.'

Cardboard, thought Alex. Why did burning cardboard ring a bell? It came to him. 'Paulo, remember that gamekeeper at the lodge who made a fuss about the ketamine box? He said he was going to make a bonfire. What if he was going to come up here and burn it? What if this is where they get rid of the evidence?'

He squatted down beside Paulo to look.

Paulo scraped at the pieces of melted plastic but

they were fused to the hearth. 'They've been burning this too. They've cut up something. Maybe more packaging. Doesn't look like it burns very well.'

Alex went back to searching the other end of the bothy. 'That still isn't very much. It's not worth locking the place for.'

Paulo straightened up and looked further along the wall beyond the chimney. There was mortar dust on the floor. And shards of stone. As if something had scraped the wall. He looked carefully up the outside of the stone chimney. One of the stones looked loose.

He pulled it out and mortar dust sprinkled down. He'd have to be careful not to leave signs he'd been there. A nice footprint would certainly give the game away. He reached in with his fingers. And touched a wooden box. 'Alex!'

Alex hurried over as Paulo brought out the box and laid it on the floor. It was about the size of a box of tissues. The top was scraped as if it was taken out and replaced frequently.

Paulo lifted the lid. Inside were pale rubber gloves and green surgical masks.

Then he saw Alex's face change. '*Hombre*, are you OK?'

Alex nodded slowly. Suddenly he remembered what he had seen; the missing piece of his experience while he was drugged. His voice came out as a whisper. 'This is what I saw. This is what's been bothering me all this time. When I saw the men in here that night they were wearing masks and gloves. But you don't need masks and gloves to gut deer.'

'But,' said Paulo, 'you do need them if you're pouring large quantities of dusty pills into bags. They must bring the pills up here in the carcasses then decant them into smaller packets for distribution.'

'These must be covered in evidence,' said Alex. 'Dust from whatever drugs they've been decanting. We can bring the police up to search the place.'

There was a sharp rap on the door. Alex looked at Paulo, then jumped up and went to see who it was.

Several things flashed through Alex's mind. Had they been caught? No. The gamekeepers wouldn't knock. A knock was the sound of someone who believed he was on someone else's patch, not someone who had found intruders. So Alex could behave like he was meant to be there. He heard the clop of wood on wood as Paulo put the lid on the box.

Alex pulled the door open.

Outside was a man with a silvered beard and a red Gore-Tex walker's jacket. Around his neck was a pair of high-powered binoculars. He held out an Ordnance Survey map.

'Sorry to disturb you. I wonder if you could show me where exactly I am . . . I'm not very good with a map.'

'Let's see if I can help,' said Alex. He took the map and got his compass out of his pocket.

Meanwhile Paulo inspected the fireplace. There was a print from the toe of his boot where they had been investigating the ashy remains. He picked up a wire brush and brushed the ash neatly into a pile again. He could hear the walker chatting to Alex.

Then, suddenly, Paulo caught a smell of something. Like burning. It must be the ashes, he thought.

But Alex spotted a curl of yellow flame behind the man. 'Better come away from the heather – the gamekeepers are burning it.' He showed the man in. It wouldn't hurt to wait in the bothy until the flames burned out, but they'd better get away soon if the gamekeepers were starting to work in the area.

Paulo stood up, and saw smoke boiling across the window, yellow curls of flame.

'Well, thanks for that,' the man was saying to Alex. 'My brother used to like coming here, but I don't know the area at all.'

'Used to?' said Alex, as he pulled the door shut. Suddenly the handle was wrenched out of his hand. The door slammed and there was a click as it was locked – from the outside.

Paulo ran to the window. He saw a moving figure, then flames flying through the air. A Molotov cocktail.

Alex launched himself at Paulo and the man and pushed them away from the window. There was a smash and glass showered down around them. A gout of flame shot up to the ceiling. The heat was fierce, like a flamethrower, and flaming liquid was spreading towards Alex's hands on the ground. He rolled away. The fumes caught in his throat: petrol.

Paulo pulled the walker to his feet. At the other end of the room the petrol river touched the wooden benches. Flames began to climb them, sizzling and spitting. They had to get out quickly. Once the benches went up the heat would be unbearable. But the window was cut off by a river of flame. The only way out was the door.

Paulo and Alex had the same thought. Together they launched themselves at it, putting all their weight against it, but it didn't budge.

The man started coughing, his eyes wide with panic. Alex took Paulo's arm and gestured towards the hiker, then fell to his knees in front of the door. Paulo stripped his black jumper off and wrenched the lid off his water bottle with his teeth. He tipped the contents over the sleeves and put one to the man's mouth. 'Breathe,' he yelled. He took the other sleeve himself.

Alex was trying to get the lock-picking probes out of his pocket but his body was racked by spasms of coughing.

'Hurry, Alex!' screamed Paulo.

'Help!' screamed the man. His cry ended in coughing.

Alex had the probe in the lock. His hands were shaking, and when he wasn't shaking, he was coughing. He couldn't feel the tumblers moving. Sweat was pouring off him and the probe was slipping in his fingers. It was becoming hot. Alex was coughing so hard he couldn't see; couldn't feel anything inside the lock; couldn't hear the tumblers.

Concentrate, he told himself. This is the only way out. Focus.

Paulo held onto the man and stared at Alex's shaking back. How could he hope to pick the lock in these conditions? It had been hard enough coming in. They were trapped. The walls of the bothy were solid and the windows were cut off by a wall of crackling flame.

There was a roar from the other end of the room. The heat increased. One of the benches had gone up in flames. Then the door swung open.

Alex fell outside, coughing. Paulo pulled the hiker out of the bothy.

It was almost as hot outside. The heather was

burning and the air was thick with smoke. Had they escaped the fire inside only to burn outside?

Alex grabbed the man's arm. He fixed him and Paulo with a purposeful look. 'Run, as fast as you can, after me.'

He turned and took off through the burning heather. If he kept moving swiftly he might avoid being caught. The heather spat and crackled around him and he felt its heat. He had to keep running. Ahead was a clear area, where the heather had already been burned and the fire had died down. The flames couldn't reach him here. He bent over, dragging air into his ravaged lungs. He was safe. Where were the others?

Paulo was running hard. The man was behind him, his binoculars swinging, his red jacket flying out behind him. He was keeping up – surprising considering he was well into his fifties. But that was what panic did to you.

Paulo realized Alex had stopped. He fell to his knees and for a few moments just stayed there, breathing, thankful that he was alive. Behind him the hiker dropped to the ground and rolled to and fro on his back. Paulo started towards him, but the man was soon sitting up, brushing at a burned hole in his jacket and coughing. He'd been on fire but he'd managed to put it out.

'Nice one,' coughed Paulo.

Alex was looking carefully at the man. Inhaling smoke and fumes could be almost as dangerous as burn injuries. 'Are you OK?' he asked.

The hiker nodded. 'Just catching my breath.' He coughed again, but his face was pink and his lips were a healthy colour – not the bluish pallor of someone poisoned by smoke.

Behind, through the smoke and the crackling heather, they saw orange flames leaping out of the window and open door of the bothy and licking through one of the roof trusses. Alex swallowed, realizing they had got out just in time.

'Is everyone all right?' said Paulo.

Alex nodded, and coughed; the hiker was coughing again too.

'Should we try to contain the fire?' asked Paulo.

The flames near them were dying, leaving twisted clumps of black heather.

'I think it'll sort itself out,' said Alex. 'It's a natural process.'

'That Molotov cocktail wasn't a natural process,' said the hiker. 'That was arson. We'd better report it to the police. I never thought you'd get vandalism out here.'

Alex got out his mobile. He was surprised to see it wasn't damaged. But there was no signal here. He looked again at the bothy.

Beside him Paulo sighed. His breath wheezed slightly.

All the evidence was going up in smoke.

18

TARGETS

Hex walked slowly through the wiry grass of the moor, looking at his palmtop screen. He took a final pace and stopped. 'It's here somewhere.'

Amber took something out of her rucksack and unfolded it. It was a pole with a disc on one end: a metal detector. Paulo had found it in the loft at the hostel. It hadn't been working, but he had dismantled it and found a loose connection. Then he asked Li if he could borrow her opal ring. He tossed it away onto the gravel drive, then gleefully found it with the machine. Li was only mildly grateful.

Li looked at the open moor. She remembered very well the faint outline of light around her hands and knees but she couldn't see any sign of the trapdoor now. 'I can't see it,' she sighed. 'Try the gizmo.'

Amber switched the metal detector on. It made a low humming noise and a red LED winked. As she walked towards Hex it started to bleep. 'There's metal here,' she said. She swung it away; it still bleeped. 'It seems to think there's metal everywhere.'

Hex frowned. 'Maybe there is. Try it over there.'

Amber took it to where the ground sloped away. The beeping stopped.

'OK, I've got to the edge.' Amber began to walk in a straight line away from the other two. The bleeping started again. 'There's something buried here,' she said. 'Something big.' The bleeping stopped, then started again at a right angle to the first line.

In the distance, just over one of the hills, a plume of black smoke was rising. 'Funny,' said Li, 'they're out burning the heather early today.'

Hex followed her gaze. 'I didn't think heather made as much smoke as that.' He looked at Amber.

Li giggled.

Amber came back brandishing the metal detector like a weapon. 'There's something big and metal under here. I'd say it's about twenty metres by ten.' She switched off the machine and folded it up again.

'And it's metal?' said Li. 'Why would it be metal?'

'Shh – what's that?' said Hex.

It was the sound of an engine.

'I'm no expert,' said Amber, 'but that sounds like a quad bike.'

'The gamekeepers,' said Hex. 'We'd better get out of here.'

The six-wheel ATV crested the hill. A figure stood upright behind the driver. His posture was unmistakable – head to one side, looking along a barrel. A shot rang out.

Li felt the ground explode by her heel. She did the only thing she could – run.

Hex and Amber took off in zigzagging lines behind her. If they gave the shooter several targets, it might slow him up. Amber rolled into a gulley. She heard shouts and a rifle bolt being pulled back. She started to pull herself along in the water in case they'd seen her go in. Hex followed her down, then Li quickly tumbled in after him. They were all like soldiers in a trench.

The stream bed made a narrow channel like a miniature canyon. Hex began to pull himself along on his elbows. The others followed, crawling as fast as possible. They might as well move while they could.

They heard the ATV's engine rev. Good, that would cover any sound they made. Hex got up on hands and knees and stepped up the pace. Amber and Li were right behind him.

Suddenly he stopped as he saw the end of the stream bed. 'It's a dead end,' he hissed. 'They know we're in here. We need to get out.'

Li cautiously peered out and nearly had heart failure. Right by her nose was a pair of sturdy walking boots and argyle socks. The gamekeepers weren't both on the ATV any more. The one with the gun was right here.

Too late to retreat. Li took her courage in her hands. She exploded out of the gulley and knocked the gamekeeper over. His gun went off and she twisted it out of his hands and threw it away like a javelin. He grabbed at her leg but she gave him a vicious kick on the chin.

The others darted out of the trench. The gamekeeper on the ATV gave chase. Amber saw a steep slope and headed down it. Hex hared after her and Li followed close behind.

Another shot whistled past Hex's ear. He caught a glimpse of a man at the top of the slope, ready to fire. The gamekeeper must have retrieved his gun. The ATV droned behind him. Maybe the man wouldn't fire with the ATV in the way. But now the vehicle was their main problem, not the gun.

Amber was in front. Hex moved away from Li. If they stayed together they presented an easy target. With several of them moving in different directions, it was more confusing.

The slope was getting steeper. Li needed all her balance not to fall over. Suddenly she heard the whine of the engine and the bounce of the axles right behind her. The ATV had given up on Hex and Amber and was now after her. She felt its wheels pushing the long grass onto her calves and leaped to the side. She was too vulnerable on her own.

The slope fell away even more steeply. Li ran back towards Hex and Amber, using her hand to keep herself upright. The ATV had slowed, but so had they. And what was Amber doing?

Amber veered back up the hill, climbing on all fours. The ATV swerved and the wheels on one side left the ground. As Amber watched it, she could see that the driver's pockmarked face was pure panic. Abandon ship, she thought. Just step off. If you stay on, it will fall over and crush you.

But the ATV bounced back onto six wheels. Damn, thought Amber. Then the driver stopped and took out a weapon. A sawn-off shotgun.

Hex ran in from the side and elbowed him roughly off the vehicle; the shotgun spun through the air. While Li leaped onto the flat bed at the back, Hex pressed the throttle switch and turned the handlebars so they were pointing straight downhill. Li hooked her arms under Amber's shoulders and hauled her on.

'Go go go, Hex!' shrieked Amber.

A shot rang over their heads but Hex opened the throttle to full. If they went in a straight line they could go at the vehicle's top speed. He lay back on the seat, his feet on the foot rests, trying to keep his balance. Behind him Li's and Amber's heads bumped against his. But they were getting away.

However, the slope wasn't smooth and Hex wrestled to keep the handlebars pointing straight downhill. The wheels clattered loudly on the chassis; if they started to go at the slightest angle, the machine would tip over for sure. He didn't know how Li and Amber were staying on but he prayed they wouldn't let go.

The girls were spread-eagled on the flat bed, hands and feet hooked onto whatever they could get hold of. Amber had an excellent view of the fat tyres, spinning crazily. Li was clinging to her. She was terrified she would slip and knock Hex off. The ground went past in a bouncing, rib-battering blur.

A shot rang out. They weren't out of danger yet. Hex kept his thumb on the throttle. The speedometer was climbing steadily. Now it said 66 kph. Some small compartment of Hex's brain that loved numbers gave a little smile: that was about 10 kph above the vehicle's top speed. With this slope they must be breaking records.

Suddenly Hex realized he couldn't see the ground ahead. There just seemed to be a kind of shelf, and then some more grass a little further away. They were heading for a sheer drop.

Hex squeezed the brake. It made little difference. After all, they were doing record-breaking speed. The edge came up fast. There was nothing he could do. 'Hold tight!' he yelled.

He stood up in the foot rests like a jockey and hoped for the best.

Li and Amber found they were looking down on water. For a moment they seemed to hang there, like a gliding bird.

The impact was like hitting a wall. A great wave of freezing water engulfed them. Hex felt himself going over the handlebars. He clung on and his arms nearly came out of their sockets. There were muffled cries from behind.

Underneath him, the bike slowed and bounced. The tidal wave settled and Hex found himself standing on his foot rests, up to his waist in the icy water of a river, with the engine still running.

He looked behind him. Amber was pulling Li back onto the flat bed. Li's cheek was bleeding.

'Nice one, Hex,' said Li, breathing hard.

Amber was panting. 'What now?'

Hex looked up at the mountain. They had left wavy tracks like a double pinstripe down the hill, but there was no sign of the gamekeepers. He slowed to a stop and cut the engine. 'We've lost them. Maybe we should leave the bike here and continue on foot.'

He tried to get off, but his legs had turned to jelly after the effort of holding his position on the bike. Amber started to let go of the flat bed, but her fingers wouldn't obey. She had to uncurl them slowly. Li let out a long, slow breath and tumbled off the ATV.

They splashed through the water onto the river bank.

As soon as they climbed out onto dry land Hex was checking the GPS.

'Where are we?' asked Amber.

Hex grinned. 'Well, we've travelled approximately

four hundred metres from where the factory is. Vertically.'

Li circled her arms. 'Yes, I realize that.' She grimaced and the cut on her cheek squeezed out a tear of blood.

Hex looked up. The ground formed a natural ridge. 'If we stay in close to the ridge we should be out of sight from above.'

'Better hurry,' said Amber. 'They could easily follow us.'

She forced herself into a jog and the others followed. They were tired and aching, but it was vital that they put as much distance as possible between themselves and the gamekeepers.

Paulo opened the front door of the hostel. 'Well, poor Martin Fletcher's had a day to remember,' he said. He and Alex had been with the hiker to the police station to report the arson attack on the bothy. The police took statements and said they would send officers to inspect the site, but it was clear they were treating it as a simple case of vandalism.

From the kitchen came sounds of activity. Alex shrugged off his Gore-Tex jacket and hung it on the peg. 'Let's go and see if the others found anything.'

They were shocked at what they saw: Amber was dabbing antiseptic on a cut below Li's eye; Hex was stretching his legs and arms as though his joints had seized up; and Amber's fingers were wrapped in plasters.

'What on earth have you been up to?' said Hex. 'You smell like a bonfire.'

'You look like you've been in a bullfight,' said Paulo. 'All three of you.' He pulled out a chair and sat down. 'Do you want to go first or shall we?'

They briefly summarized the events of the morning. Alex felt drained: it was good to sit down. Suddenly he had a thought. He sat bolt upright.

'What's the matter?' said Li.

'I don't think we should be here,' he said. 'Look at us. Yesterday the gamekeepers were minding their own business, keeping their heads down. Now, they're defending their patch. They've shot at us and tried to burn us to death.'

Outside, tyres crunched on the gravel.

19

REVENGE

The five friends ran out to the hall and grabbed rucksacks and boots. Hex rushed back and snatched up the map.

Outside, the car braked and threw a spray of pebbles at the front door.

'Out through the back,' said Amber, and led the way into the office.

Paulo raised the sash window and hopped out; the others followed. They heard the front door splinter as it was kicked open.

'Down,' hissed Alex. As they crouched down

below the windowsill, footsteps echoed in the flagstoned hall.

A voice said, 'Try the kitchen.' The footsteps disappeared down the corridor.

Hex glanced up. In the window of the office he saw the reflection of figures moving through the hall. There were three of them. The one who had spoken was tall and wore a rough jumper and a blue-green kilt; one shoulder was hidden by the door frame. Then he moved and Hex saw something else. A stubby weapon.

Hex mimed holding a gun. Alex nodded. Sweat was running down his armpits and back.

Alex looked up at the hill that rose steeply behind the hostel. They couldn't get away up there. It would be too slow and they would be easy targets.

They heard voices again: the man was coming back. Alex pointed along the outside wall down towards the kitchen. Paulo crawled quickly down to the end of the building and stopped under the kitchen window. As Alex, in the rear, moved away from the office he heard the men coming in. They had got away just in time. Thank goodness the gravel didn't extend round the back of the building; here the ground was bare earth, easy to walk on silently.

They looked round the corner of the building. A battered red Ford Escort stood in the drive. It had a crumpled bonnet as though it had been used as a battering ram.

Hex spoke quietly. 'The Range Rover. It's in the garage so we'll have cover while we get in.'

Alex nodded, but Paulo shook his head. 'The keys are in the house. I'll have to hotwire it. It's got an immobilizer so it'll take ages.'

'How long?' said Hex.

'About fifteen minutes. Damn.'

'Are you sure?' asked Hex. 'The immobilizer wasn't working last week.'

Paulo winced. 'I know it's working now because I fixed it the other day.' He looked at the red Escort. 'I could hotwire that in thirty seconds flat.'

Alex shook his head. 'Too risky. They might see you.'

'They won't need to see you, they'll hear you,' said Li. She pointed to the gravel.

Paulo sighed. 'We'll have to hotwire the quads. But we need all three and by the time they'd heard the first one they'd be coming down.'

Amber said, 'You tell us what to do and we'll start them all together.'

'That's what we'll have to do,' said Alex. 'Hex, what weapons did you see?'

'Sawn-off shotguns.'

'Right,' said Alex. 'Not very accurate at a distance. If they shoot from an upstairs window they probably won't get us. But we'll try not to make any noise. Ready?'

Four heads nodded back at him.

'Alex, are you OK at the back?'

Alex nodded and watched as Paulo led the group along the edge of the gravel, running silently on the hard-baked earth. The garage was a big building alongside the hostel, butting up close to the steep slope behind.

Alex followed at the back. It was only a short distance but it seemed like the longest run of his life. He felt so exposed. Each moment he expected to hear the crack of gunfire. Sawn-off shotguns.

Weapons of the underworld. He kept telling himself, They aren't accurate at that range, but he could almost feel the shot spraying into his flesh.

In less than twenty seconds he felt the solid wall of the garage building against his back. At last he could breathe easily.

Paulo looked round the front of the building. The garage door was open. He could see the three quad bikes and the dark green Range Rover. The others were behind him, waiting for his signal. He nodded and they darted round the corner and into the garage.

Paulo wasted no time. He unfastened the tool kit he carried on his belt, went up to the first quad and jammed a screwdriver into the housing that covered the ignition system. Hex saw what he was doing, grabbed a large screwdriver from a rack on the wall and did the same with the next bike. The red cover clattered to the floor as Hex did the same to the third one. Meanwhile Li, Amber and Alex grabbed what they could: Amber and Li took loops of rope and hung them over their bodies diagonally; Alex reached into the Range Rover and pulled out a couple of rucksacks. He threw one to Hex and put one on himself. They were emergency supplies in case they got stranded on the moors.

Amber could see someone else was needed on the third quad and climbed into the driver's seat. Paulo passed a couple of nails to Hex, and Hex passed one to Amber. Li got on behind Amber while Alex got on the back of the middle bike, behind Hex.

Paulo straddled the first bike. 'See the two little things that look like metal flowers? When I tell you, put the nail across them so that the little pointy things in the middle are connected. That will crank the engine. Then get out as fast as possible.'

Two faces watched him, serious.

'Three, two, one – now!'

In perfect unison, the three quad bikes spluttered into life. Paulo immediately reversed his out; Hex nearly cannoned into him; Amber took hers wider and roared off onto the drive, her wheels spraying gravel up like water.

They were right not to hang around. Two shots rang out from one of the upper windows. All five friends ducked, the drivers lying almost flat on the handlebars as they roared away.

Paulo looked for a spot to leave the road. The quads weren't road legal, and anyway the gamekeepers would soon be after them in their car. On the road, the car was much faster.

The road turned a corner. Paulo stood in the foot rests and swerved his bike round hard, onto the grass and up. Behind him, he heard the noise of the bikes change as the others did the same. But a manoeuvre like that would have left marks on the road. They had to vanish without a trace.

Paulo gunned the throttle and the bike climbed up and over the crest of a hill and then down again. They were off the skyline now. They could take a breather. He braked.

Amber pulled up alongside. 'I know somewhere we can hide,' she said. 'Follow me.'

A gentle pattering of rain started as Amber led the way into the ruined barn she had found when they were looking for Tiff.

It was just about big enough for three quad bikes.

Half of the roof was still there and they managed to manoeuvre the bikes under cover. And it got them out of sight.

Paulo looked up at the sky. 'Well, the rain should help cover our tracks.'

Amber slumped in her quad seat, exhausted. 'That was horrible. They would have shot us. Alex, you must have sixth sense.'

Alex looked stunned too. 'I suddenly thought – that hostel is owned by the laird. The gamekeepers knew where to find us.'

Hex kept seeing the figure mirrored in the window; the brutal sawn-off shotgun. He suddenly sat up, alert. 'What if these bikes have got tracers on them? We hired them from the laird. I wouldn't rent out vehicles without making sure I could trace where they were.'

'You're right.' Alex jumped up. 'They don't need to search for us, just track us. We'd better get moving.' He swung the rucksack off his back, pulled out five pairs of thin waterproof trousers and handed them around. Swiftly they put them on.

Outside the rain came down harder; the kind of drenching storm you only got in summer.

Hex had the map he rescued from the kitchen and Alex checked the compass from his survival tin. 'Best to head up as high as possible,' he said.

They climbed up on top of the ridge fairly quickly. The rain brought the noise of traffic from the road far below. Three jets screamed overhead, making the five friends jump. Alex broke into a run. He was too wound up to keep still. Like spooked deer, the others followed. They ran up the slope and off into the hills.

After a good twenty minutes Alex slowed to a walk. They had probably gone far enough for now. The rain was teeming down, but they were warm from running.

'They obviously intended to sort us out,' said Hex. His short hair was even more spiky than usual in the rain. 'What will they do now?'

Paulo said, 'Maybe if they can't find us, they'll cut their losses and run. Before the police close in.'

'If they do that,' said Li, 'they've got a big bad dealer who'll come after them. I saw that guy and they are scared of him. I think they'll do the deal before they get out.'

'I saw a tall guy in a kilt,' said Hex. 'Not one of the gamekeepers. There are more of them than we think.'

'What did he look like?'

'I don't know. I only saw him from behind.'

Rain was dripping down Amber's nose. She wiped it away. 'Hey, guys, reality check. Things have changed. Those gamekeepers are now out for our blood. We should go straight to the police.'

'No,' said Alex.

Amber stopped walking and stared at Alex. 'No?'

Alex looked away into the distance, as if thinking. 'The police don't know where to find them. They've got the whole of this estate to search. The gamekeepers know every inch and they'll probably get away – and then what? We might be safe in the short term, but there are a bunch of drug dealers out there with a score to settle. We don't know if we'll ever run into them again, but if we do our lives will be in danger.'

'We've got to put them behind bars,' said Li.

'For a long time,' added Paulo. 'So we need the police to see all the evidence *and* catch all the dealers.'

Alex knew he was right, but he wanted to make sure everyone was with him on this. 'Hex, what do you think?'

'It's a no-brainer,' said Hex. 'We go to the police now and look over our shoulders for the rest of our lives. We wait a few hours and set up a nice trap, and then we can all sleep easily. I say we have to stick to our plan.'

Alex looked at Amber again.

Amber nodded. 'I've had school friends whose lives were ruined by drugs. And do you know what? I don't like being threatened by guns. Let's put them away.'

They started walking again slowly, still lost in thought. Over the top of a ridge they came to a single-track road. As they crossed it they took advantage of the view and looked carefully in both directions. The only moving things were two bedraggled Highland cattle in the distance, swishing their tails in the rain.

'Next question,' said Alex. 'Where do we go from here? How do we find out when the buyers are coming?'

'We need two teams,' said Hex. 'One to go close in, follow them around at the lodge, and one to stay hidden in the field. Which of us can they identify?'

Alex thought. 'They might have seen me up close in the bothy this morning. I don't know how long they were watching us for. Paulo, they'll have seen you too.'

'They could identify me anyway,' said Paulo. 'They saw me that day when I caught their pony.' He turned to the others. 'How close did you get to them at the factory?'

'It's hard to say,' said Amber. 'We were all running around. I certainly didn't get a good look at them, so maybe they didn't get a close look at us.'

'I gave one of them a good kicking,' said Li. 'I don't think he'll forget me. And I was there when the pony bolted.'

'What about that day when we took the dog into the yard?' said Amber. 'They must have seen all of us. Alex, you talked to one of them, when he wanted the ketamine box.'

'Yes, but I'm out of the close surveillance team anyway,' said Alex. 'Did he talk to anyone else?'

'He was looking at all of us,' said Paulo.

'But it was at a distance, right?' said Hex. 'With a complete change of clothes and context, there are two of us who could maybe slip past them unnoticed.' He stopped and unfolded the map.

'You're forgetting something,' said Amber. 'I'm gonna stick out like a sore thumb at the lodge. There aren't many black people in this part of Scotland.'

Hex shook his head. 'Except for that celebrity singer and all her friends who are staying there. The lodge is over-run with sassy black Americans. Just dress like them and you could easily be part of her entourage.'

'I'm not part of anyone's entourage,' sniffed Amber.

'We don't have to stay there long, so a superficial disguise is fine. We find out when the delivery is scheduled, tell the others and get out.'

'We?' said Amber dubiously. 'You think they'll let you into a place like that?'

Hex grimaced. 'I promise not to drink the fingerbowls.'

Alex recapped the plan so far. 'OK, so you two are

in the lodge. You get the information. Meanwhile we'll go to ground on the moors and check out the factory in detail.'

Li said, 'I think we should take a closer look at the stalagmite cave too. It's very close and we never explored properly underground – I did hear the generator from there. There could be other tunnels nearby and they might have an escape route.'

The others nodded in agreement.

'How,' asked Hex, 'are you going to pick up a mobile signal from there? Most of the moors are dead zones.'

Four blank faces looked back at him.

Hex unclipped the palmtop from his belt and handed it to Alex. 'I got an upgrade this morning. It uses a communications satellite to bounce signals off the nearest phone cell. Sort of a hacker's version of a satellite phone on a ship. When we've got the information, we'll give you a call.'

Alex took the palmtop almost reverently. 'I'll take good care of it.'

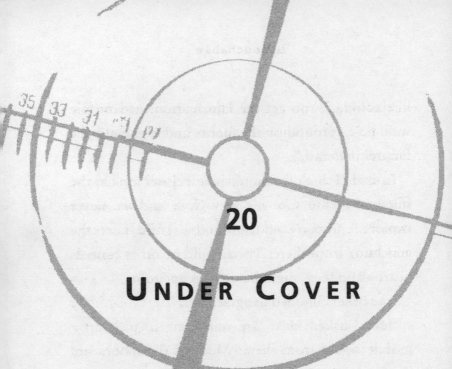

20

UNDER COVER

'Reservation for two,' said Amber. 'My agent phoned you last week about it . . . No, you've made a mistake.'

Hex looked in the window of the Glaickvullin country clothing shop. The space where his palmtop usually was felt very empty, like a missing tooth. He never went anywhere without it. And the window display was faintly disorientating. Gleaming, polished rifles rested on a background of green and blue tartan, overlooked by a stuffed jay. It was a dead bird and a couple of guns, but it was trying to look like a cosy Christmas card. Hex remembered the last time he'd seen guns – just that morning. Rather a different story.

Amber was different too. 'Don't tell me you've filled every room,' she said into the phone. Gone was the girl who squirmed through muddy ditches and hung onto ATVs for dear life. Here was rich-bitch Amber, bullying Glaickvullin Lodge to give her a room. 'Two singles in a suite. That'll do.' She cut the connection.

Hex looked at her. 'Is this wise? Wasn't the hostel booked in the name of Middleton?'

Amber shook her head. 'It was booked as Adventure Tours dot com. They can't link me to them through my credit card. If we're guests, we can get through a lot more doors than if we're grubby vagabonds who've wandered in off the moor.' She linked her arm through his.

Hex realized she was propelling him towards the door of the shop. 'We're going in there?' he exclaimed.

'We need a superficial disguise.'

Inside, the shop was deeply carpeted. A wooden

cabinet stood opposite the entrance, the drawers stacked with silk ties and handkerchiefs. A small assemblage of dummies wore complete tweed shooting outfits.

Amber grabbed a pale creamy yellow flat cap from a dummy and pulled it onto her head. Then she spotted something else and stopped suddenly. Hex nearly ran into her. 'Wow, look at this.' She handed him a black leather riding boot, running her fingers over the shiny contoured leg with an expression of awe. 'Feel this. They're handmade in Argentina. Aren't they divine?'

Hex didn't need to feel the boot, he could smell it. It smelled like the interior of an expensive car. He caught sight of the price tag and nearly fainted: £950!

Close by his elbow, a black-clad assistant said, 'We can have them added to your bill, if you're staying at the lodge.'

Hex shook his head and was about to give the boot back to Amber, but she had moved on, rummaging through a rack of clothes, making selections at lightning speed. It was like watching a

Special Operations ambush – swift and effective. The assistant hovered, ready to help, but saw that Amber knew what she was doing.

Amber straightened up. 'Come and try these on.' She didn't need to be shown the way to the changing rooms: she had already sussed the shop's layout.

Hex followed, bewildered. A swish of a curtain and he found himself inside a room as big as his entire bedroom at home. A plush velvet-upholstered chair sat waiting for his discarded clothes. The last changing room he'd been in had been a poky cupboard with a plastic chair.

On a rack were the clothes Amber had picked out. He lifted up a frock coat made from green tweed criss-crossed with fine purple lines like graph paper. It looked like something Prince Philip would wear. How could she do this to him? Next door he heard rustlings and the smart buzz of a zip. Amber's voice fluttered over the partition. She was next door.

'Honey, I don't hear much changing going on.'

Hex sighed. It was clothes for a mission, not to make him feel like himself. He pulled off his black O'Neill fleece, picked up a checked shirt and winced.

He came out wearing green plus-fours in a lightweight summer tweed, matching long green socks and his walking boots. He barely recognized Amber. She was dressed virtually the same but had made it look trendy – green plus-fours except a size too big so they hung around her hips like cropped cargo pants, and a long, tight-fitting tweed waistcoat that emphasized her narrow waist. The corn-coloured flat cap gave it an appealingly roguish look. She looked expensive and chic – and a good few years older. If the gamekeepers were looking for a bunch of kids, they certainly wouldn't recognize her.

Hex looked down gloomily at his own legs. 'Not sure about the plus-fours.'

Amber shook her head. 'Try the moleskins.'

Hex heard the sound of fingers on a keyboard. On the glass counter, above racks of gloves, was a computer. The assistant tapped in a password, then pushed the keyboard towards him. 'Would you like to try our tartan research database? Just type in your family name and we can find out what the most appropriate tartan is for you.'

Hex took the keyboard and had a quick look at the menus. If the computer could send bills to the lodge, it must be part of a network.

The assistant hovered. 'You just type your name in here.'

Amber realized that Hex had plans for the screen in front of him if only he could be left alone. She pulled a jacket out of a rack. 'Can you help me find what he needs to wear with a kilt?'

The assistant was only too happy to join her.

On the screen was a man in full formal Scottish evening dress – bow tie, silver-buttoned jacket, sporran and kilt with criss-crossed lines of green, red and yellow on a background of pale dusty blue. Hex crashed it and he vanished. Now, he thought, let's go for a wander around the server – have a look at the Glaickvullin Lodge accounts.

Amber watched patiently while the assistant took her through a selection of bow ties. Out of the corner of her eye she watched Hex, typing away furiously.

'What kind of dress shirt does he like?' said the assistant.

'I don't know,' said Amber. She pulled two down off the shelf and held them out. 'Hey, honey, do you like this?'

Hex looked up. 'Not quite me.'

Amber wasn't surprised. It had a double line of lacy frills down the front like cream on top of a gateau.

Hex put his head on one side, thinking. 'Have you got something plain? Or black?'

'I'll have to see what we've got in the back,' said the assistant.

Hex's eyes bored into the screen, making the most of the minutes while the assistant was out of the room and he didn't have to disguise what he was doing.

She soon came back, saying, 'We don't seem to have any in your size. I can order some for you.'

Amber realized with horror that the assistant was heading for the computer. She had to distract her. She seized a tweed jacket off a rack and swung it at her. 'Does this come in medium?'

The assistant turned round. 'I'll have a look for you,' she said, and went into the back of the shop again.

Amber breathed a sigh of relief. Crisis averted. Hex mouthed at her, 'Nearly done.'

'I think we're out of stock of those as well. I can order one and have it sent up to the lodge,' the assistant told them.

'Oh – shame,' said Amber. 'We're not staying long.'

Hex turned the screen round with a flourish. 'I've found my tartan.'

Li crawled along the narrow tunnel to the stalagmite cave, hauling herself up with the tiny handholds. Her fingers were hardened from her years of free climbing, but she had put on her gloves. Every resource they carried was vital now, and they couldn't afford to use their precious water on washing grit out of wounds.

Her head felt vulnerable – they hadn't had time to pack helmets. It was just lucky they'd managed to grab the ropes, otherwise they wouldn't have managed the abseil down into the cave entrance. Nor did they have knee pads, so they had improvised some out of T-shirts, cutting the material into strips with

Alex's knife and wrapping them around her knees. But at least they had their waterproofs and torches. It would have been very miserable without them.

She reached the elbow in the tunnel. She called back, 'I'm starting my descent now.'

'OK,' came Paulo's and Alex's voices. It was good to hear they were close.

She squirmed along, her torch in her right hand. The patch of light kept jumping around. No helmet also meant no headlight. She peered down into the tunnel below her – how much further? Were there stalagmites ahead yet?

Finally the torch picked out a faint glitter. She called back again, 'I'm at the cave.'

Paulo's voice came back, echoing: 'OK.'

She jumped down to the floor and looked around. There it was, as she remembered. The jagged, glittering stalagmites, sticking up from the uneven floor like teeth in a shark's mouth. The drip, drip of water and the occasional rasp of pebbles moving. But not the other noise. The generator wasn't on. That meant the men weren't in there. It was safe to look around – for now.

According to the cavern plan Li had memorized, the far wall was the nearest point to the buried factory. So that was where she needed to explore. She picked her way round the edge of the cave. It was like tiptoeing round a room filled with sharp ornaments. She reached the far wall and the cave roof opened up into a hole.

A cold light breeze touched her right ear and the top of her head. A draught meant a hole. Li ran her torch over the rock wall. It went on up, beyond where her light could reach. What was it? A shaft? Only one way to find out where it went. She would have to climb.

The rock was quite smooth, but her experienced eye picked out a few hand- and footholds. She'd definitely need her bare fingers, though. She peeled off her gloves and put them in her pocket, then felt the wall. How would she hold the torch? Could she climb in the pitch dark?

She would have to. Her fingers closed on the switch. They wouldn't obey her. She didn't want to turn off the torch, feel the darkness close in.

She tried shutting her eyes. There, that was

what the dark was like. It would be no worse than that.

She switched off the torch and slipped it into her pocket. Then she opened her eyes and tilted her head up.

Far above, there was a tiny patch of light. It was about the size of a coin, but it was a patch of light nevertheless. It was a way out, near the factory. She definitely had to investigate.

Li gave her fingers a quick stretch and clenched her fists a few times to get the circulation going. Then she put her hands on the wall.

Once she started, a kind of calm settled on her. Concentration drove all fears out of her head. She just went steadily up.

The tunnel became narrower, until the rough rock wall touched her back. She leaned into it and pushed herself up with her legs. The patch of light became bigger and the draught of fresh air was getting stronger, banishing the smell of wet rock and mud.

There was something else: one edge of the hole was straight and smooth. Li reached the top and found a grey plastic drainpipe ran across the top of the shaft like a bridge. By the drainpipe was a ledge. Li pulled herself up and stretched her aching limbs. Above her was a small crack in the rock, about fifteen centimetres wide — far too small to climb through, but big enough to let light in.

The drainpipe came horizontally out of the crack and went down a tunnel. Li shone her torch down it. It was wide enough to crawl down on hands and knees. Well, she might as well see where it went.

Suddenly her torch picked out a dead squirrel; it had died quite recently, she thought. It must have fallen down the fissure. She pushed it aside with her elbow. Under it were dead beetles. She looked around. The tunnel was littered with dead squirrels, field mice and voles.

This was odd. She might have expected to find one or two dead creatures, but all these? And what was this pipe?

Alex waved his arms and paced up and down the tunnel to get warm. He'd actually had a mad moment when he'd been excited about going into hiding. He didn't envy Hex and Amber their upmarket lodge. Living off the land was far more his style. After all, his dream for the trip was cooking mussels and cockles in a fire pit on the shore of the Kyle. But waiting for Li in a dark, freezing tunnel was something else.

Even Paulo, who had a high threshold for discomfort and cold, was stamping his feet. He looked at his watch. 'I wonder where she is.'

'She's only been gone about fifteen minutes,' said Alex.

'If something happens to her, how do we get her out?' asked Paulo.

Paulo didn't normally worry like this, thought Alex. The cold and dark must be getting to him too. But all they could do was sit and wait. 'At least down here we're not likely to run into the gamekeepers,' he said. 'But this third man we've seen bothers me. Who is he?'

'I've been thinking about that,' said Paulo. 'I've got a theory. Those gamekeepers seem to have the run of the place. They can burn down a bothy if they want to. They broke down the front door of the hostel and if they'd shot us in there, there would have been a hell of a lot to explain. They didn't seem worried that anyone would find out. They can do what they like on the laird's land, they're untouchable. And why? Because the laird is also in on it.'

Alex spoke slowly. 'So you think the guy with the kilt that Hex saw – was the laird?'

Paulo nodded.

21

THE LAIRD'S
KINGDOM

The pheasant pens looked like tennis courts, roofed over with netting. 'Predators are a problem so we keep the birds in these pens.' The laird's accent had a faint trace of London's East End, but in his blue-green kilt with walking boots and a rough army-style jumper, he looked the part as he showed newly arrived guests around the shooting facilities.

Hex was staring at the laird's kilt, until Amber nudged him to look at the birds. He glanced around. Birds scratched around the muddy earth floor, pecked at grain, shook the recent rain from their feathers and stared apprehensively at the group of humans watching them through the fence. Two middle-aged couples were also in the party.

Hex turned away from the pen. 'That bird's looking at your hat,' he said.

'Then he knows good style,' replied Amber. She was still wearing the low-slung plus-fours and corn-coloured cap. Hex had rejected the plus-fours and gone for a checked shirt and distressed jeans. The 'distressing' was absurdly modest – a small hole on the thigh darned by a Jermyn Street tailor.

'Hey, a fellow American? Where are you from?'

'Boston, Massachusetts.' Amber shook hands with the two couples. Their tweed skirts and trousers had knife-edge creases, as though they had only recently been taken off the hangers in the shop.

'OK,' called the laird. 'That's all there is to see outside. It's time to go in and I'll show you the gun store.'

He led the way with easy strides across the yard. They dodged round staff members going to and from the farm buildings. Earlier on the tour, the laird had shown them the feed room, with tall steel bins containing sweet-smelling grain, the fertilizer room, where drums of organic fertilizer stood bearing hazard stickers. Amber glimpsed other rooms as they went past: a workshop, a rest room with a kettle and mugs, a wet clothes room with a daily timetable for checking livestock. But one door remained locked. Its paintwork was just as scarred as the others' so it was clearly used. Just not while people were watching, perhaps.

Hex was looking at the laird's kilt again. He'd seen a lot of tartans that afternoon and he'd researched one in particular. A blue-green, like that one. It was a modern design, not a traditional one. A tartan made up for tourists who wanted a piece of Scottish history but had no real ancestral links. That suggested he was trying to fit in, like a chameleon. Was he the man who had tried to kill them? Hex had only caught a brief glimpse of him.

As they headed for the back entrance, a quad bike puttered into the yard. Amber saw the missing panel first, then the rider. The gamekeeper with the pockmarked face and the scar. She looked away quickly and seized Hex's arm, nuzzling his ear.

Hex was startled, then heard her whisper, 'They've found the quads.'

'Would you just excuse me a moment, ladies and gentlemen,' said the laird. He walked over to the gamekeeper, his kilt swinging.

Hex turned and murmured in Amber's ear. 'Let's go.' They walked into the lodge through a dark passage and emerged in the main entrance hall. It was an impressive space. The staircase was huge, like Grand Central Station's, and edged with stone balustrading. Crimson leather sofas were clustered around a magnificent stone fireplace the height of a railway tunnel. One of the doors next to the fireplace swung open and a man in a butler's uniform came through, a tray containing cocktails poised on one outstretched palm.

Amber and Hex had hoped to slip away on their own, but the other guests on the tour were following.

'We've got to get rid of them,' muttered Hex.

Amber let out a lascivious giggle and hooked her arm around Hex's waist.

'I think we should leave these young people to

explore on their own,' said a woman's voice behind them.

Amber steered Hex up the stairs. 'Perhaps see you later,' chuckled one of the men.

On hands and knees, Li led Paulo and Alex down the tunnel with the drainpipe. She had found it joined up with one of the tunnels near the entrance – a much easier route than squirming through to the stalagmite cavern and up the shaft.

'It's quite long,' said Li, at the front, 'and eventually it goes into— Ah, here we are.'

She shuffled to one side and the others hunkered down beside her. The crevice above them let in light, so they switched off their torches to save the batteries.

Paulo knelt close to the drainpipe and sniffed it.

'Don't get high,' said Li.

'Diesel fumes. This is the exhaust pipe for the generator. They've been clever installing it near this pothole so they wouldn't have to build chimneys. And this is their only ventilation hole, which is why they've kept the fumes contained in this pipe.'

Alex stood up and peered into the crevice where the drainpipe disappeared. 'This is the factory?'

'It must be,' said Li. 'It's in the right place.'

'I wonder how far this crevice goes.' He switched his torch on and shone it into the hole.

'Well?' said Li.

'Can't see much . . . some bulky shapes, lots of glass pipes . . . It's really close.'

Paulo tapped him on the shoulder, offering his mobile. 'Take a picture.'

'I would if I had very long, slim fingers,' said Alex, 'but I can't reach down the hole.'

Li took off her rucksack and rummaged inside. She brought out a wire coathanger. 'How about this? It got into my bag along with my Gore-tex jacket.'

'Excellent,' said Paulo. He straightened it out and handed it to Alex.

Alex made a rough cage for the phone and set it to take several frames on a timed exposure. He passed it gently through the crevice into the container. He slid it to the limit of his reach, then heard several clicks as it took the pictures. He pulled it back out, unthreaded the case and inspected the results. A slow, satisfied smile broke out over his face. He handed the phone to Li and Paulo.

The two friends gasped.

The pictures showed red walls with steel ribs; royal-blue drums; several items of glass, like a complicated laboratory. There was no doubt – this was the underground drugs lab.

Paulo was thinking. 'You know what they do? I bet they bring the ingredients here inside the carcasses. When they get an order they take the finished product to the bothy to be counted and bagged, then transport it in a carcass to the coast.'

'Why do they bother with the bothy?' said Alex. 'They could do everything underground.'

'Ventilation?' said Paulo. He squinted at the picture. 'It looks very crowded in there. There must be a lot of dust when they're measuring pills out. The bothy's bigger, with better ventilation. Even there, we saw they had to use masks.'

Li nodded. 'It's very clever. Everything's hidden – the factory's underground and every time they move something it's inside a carcass. No one need ever see anything unusual.'

Paulo looked at the picture on the phone. 'But how long did it take them to build all this? Surely that would have attracted attention.'

'Let me see that,' said Alex. Paulo handed him the phone. Alex looked at the picture. 'Ah yes, I thought so. They didn't build it.' He pointed to the steel ribs on the walls. 'It's one of those transcontinental containers, like they carry on ships and lorries. They must have dug a great big hole and buried it. Simple and quick.'

Li nodded. 'That's why we found such a big area when we paced it out with the metal detector.'

'Those blue drums,' said Paulo. 'We found pieces of them in the bothy. They obviously contain the raw materials. I wonder where they dispose of them? They must have quite a collection.'

Li looked at her watch. 'Ten minutes and we need to go to the surface to call the others.'

Alex looked at the pipe snaking into the factory. 'This is a brilliant discovery, Li.'

Paulo nodded. His mind was already working. 'If the others can find out when the pick-up is, there's a lot we can do with this.'

22

OLD FRIEND

Hex pulled back the portcullis on the lift and stepped out into a deep-pile crimson carpet. They turned down the corridor towards their suite. It was time to call the others.

The other lift in the pair arrived and they heard a rattling sound. The iron portcullis was stiff. There was also a voice – a rather distinctive one. 'I've been abseiling, potholing, kayaking . . .'

Hex and Amber froze.

'Really?' said a male voice.

'Oh yes. My horse bolted with me on the moors

and I had to navigate off a foggy sea using just my compass.'

Hex looked at Amber with an expression of pure fear. 'Tiff,' he mouthed.

'Wow, you're a really adventurous girl,' said the male voice.

'She's showing off,' whispered Amber.

The portcullis finally snapped open.

Amber and Hex shared the same thought. They did not want to run into Tiff right now. Hex noticed a door-shaped outline running across the picture rail and down through the dado. It must be one of the secret servants' entrances. As the voices came towards them he pushed it open. Amber practically pushed him through to get out of the way in time.

They were in a windowless stone stairwell lit by a bare light bulb, in marked contrast to the opulence they had just left behind. Sounds and smells of cooking wafted up from below.

Hex looked around, curious. 'How the other half live.'

Amber pulled the door open a crack and peered back into the luxury world. 'They've gone.'

They went back into the corridor. Their suite was just a few doors along.

Amber closed the door and locked it. Now, finally, they were alone.

'What's she doing here?' spluttered Hex. He unclipped the phone from his belt and waved it around, looking for the best signal.

Amber belly-flopped onto a massive four-poster bed. Everything in their suite was on a grand scale. Their two bedrooms were each the size of an entire apartment. 'She's changed her tune.' Her voice shifted into Tiff's nasal tones. '*My stallion bolted, I navigated out of a sea fret using just my sense of smell.*' Amber's expression was furious. 'She hated every minute she spent with us. Now she's a born again Lara Croft.'

Hex needed a stronger signal and moved to the window. It was starting to rain again. 'We need to keep out of her way. She could blow our cover.'

Amber traced the pattern of the heavy brocaded bedspread with her finger. 'If she carries on boasting like that, she'll blow her own cover. If the gamekeepers hear her it'll be obvious she was at the hostel.'

Hex had a horrible thought. 'That day you rescued the dog and brought it here, she was with you. Did the gamekeepers get a good look at her?'

Amber thought. 'Only as much as they noticed me. But we're being careful, trying to stay out of their way. Tiff's broadcasting what she's been doing and where she's been doing it. What if she starts spouting about our "night orienteering"?' She looked at Hex. 'Should we warn her? She could be in danger too.'

'She wouldn't believe us. We're better trying to stay invisible. But she's a time bomb.'

Outside, the hills were covered in a shroud of fine mist as the rain came in. Hex decided that was the best signal he was going to get and dialled.

Alex was ready for the call. He, Li and Paulo stood in the shaft at the entrance to the pothole. Li and Paulo sheltered from the rain while Alex stood in the open area in the middle so the satellites in the navigation system could see him. It wasn't the only entrance, but it was the best place for staying out of sight in case there were people looking round the factory site.

Rain drummed on Alex's hood, formed rivers around his feet. Above him, the leafy fronds of summer vegetation hung over the hole, heavy with water. It was like standing at the bottom of a well.

'Hope you're keeping that thing dry,' was Hex's opening line.

'We gave it a couple of rides over the bumps in one of those narrow shafts. It's got a few scratches. How's life at the Ritz?'

'Warm and dry,' was Hex's rejoinder.

Touché, thought Alex. Serves me right for trying to wind him up.

'We lowered a camera into the factory and took some pictures. We think there's a waste dump somewhere, full of blue barrels, which might be good evidence. We found the ventilation shaft to the factory, which we think will be useful. How about you?'

'Not much yet. Except I was right about the quads having trackers. They found them.'

Alex let his breath out as a whistle. 'Well, they obviously went looking for us pretty thoroughly. You guys be careful there.'

'The laird's definitely in on it. When the

gamekeeper came back with our quad they went and had a quiet chat.'

'We thought he was too,' said Alex. 'Anything else?'

'He's covered his tracks well,' said Hex. 'I looked through the Glaickvullin Lodge accounts and it all looks squeaky clean.'

'You looked at the accounts? Maybe there are less obviously incriminating things. The factory's a transcontinental container. He must have got a JCB to dig a big hole and he must have bought the container. Was there anything like that in the accounts?'

'No,' said Hex. 'He must have paid cash.'

'Have you got that handover time yet?'

'No.'

'As soon as you do, we've got a plan. Speak to you again in an hour.' He cut the connection and crouched gratefully back into the cave.

Li shivered. 'Have they got the handover time?'

Alex shook his head.

Paulo looked at his watch. It was nearly seven o'clock. 'We've got about three hours until sundown.'

Alex took his rucksack off and walked down the

passageway in search of more shelter. 'Well, they're enjoying the high life.' He brought out an individual gas stove. 'Anyone fancy a brew?'

Hex got up from the window seat. 'They've found the factory, they've got a plan. All we've found is Tiff. We've got to step up, get active.'

'The laird's behind this, isn't he?' said Amber. 'We need to watch him in private somehow. He must have an office. Is there anywhere we can get a plan of the whole place?'

Hex went to the ornate gilded desk. Several brochures were laid out in a fan shape. He picked them up and showed them to Amber. 'There might be something in these.'

He riffled through one about the restaurant and catering. Amber took one about leisure facilities. She glanced through it while Hex opened another one. 'Hey, this one's business facilities,' he said.

He looked like he'd had an idea but Amber couldn't see the significance. 'And?'

'Conference room, ISDN facilities, broadband internet access . . . In the accounts was a bill for extending the ISDN line from the conference room to the laird's office. It wasn't that expensive, so it can't have been far. A few metres at most. I'd bet good money that the laird's private office is next door to the conference room.'

He went to his Gore-Tex jacket, which hung on its own in the cavernous wardrobe, and began taking things out of his pockets. He tossed two small silver cups onto the bed – his Bluetooth headphones. Then he unbuckled his toolkit from his belt and unrolled it.

Amber watched, none the wiser. 'So what's the plan?'

'You book the conference room. We'll need that as our operations room. Better make it for the next few hours.' He levered the cover off one of the headphones. 'I'm going to make this into a bug.'

Amber crossed to the desk to call reception. 'So one of us will have to go into the laird's office and plant it.'

Hex nodded. 'That's right.'

23

THE LION'S DEN

Amber opened the window of the conference room, letting in the smell of wet foliage and the sounds of frantic kitchen activity from the basement floor below. A cable snaked out of the window, along the wall and in through the corner of another sash window about two metres along. The window of the laird's office. How convenient, thought Amber, they've left a trail.

But its location was less convenient. Although the room was on the ground floor, the alleyway behind formed a chasm alongside the basement kitchens.

Tall, galvanized dustbins stood beside an open door. The actual drop was about five metres onto solid concrete. The only thing that connected the window she was looking out of and the laird's window was a narrow stone ledge. How slippery would it be, in the wet?

She closed the window and sat down next to Hex at the conference table.

He snapped the cover onto the bug. 'Sorry it's so big. You'll have to find something to hide it in.'

Amber slipped it into her pocket. 'So long as it works.'

'It'll work,' said Hex. 'Any speaker can be used as a microphone and vice versa. They're the same components put together in a different way.'

'And you can pick it up from here?'

'It's Bluetooth,' said Hex. 'So long as I'm within range I can hear them.'

He went with Amber to the window and looked out. 'Jeez,' he said. 'Are you sure you can make it?'

Amber's voice was resolute. 'Li would do it without turning a hair.'

Hex stepped back. His heart was in his mouth as

Amber put one leg over the sill, and then the other. She put her hand up to the open window frame, pulled herself up into a standing position and stayed there for a moment, getting her balance. Then she swung back in.

Hex caught her as she landed. 'Don't do it,' he said hurriedly. 'It's too dangerous. We'll think of something else.'

Amber shook free of his grasp and bent down to her boots. She pulled on the laces furiously. 'No I just need to take my shoes off. They're too chunky and I can't grip.' She yanked her foot out of one boot and then the other, stripped off her socks and marched back to the window.

Hex felt sick as she eased out onto the window ledge and stood up again, graceful limbs silhouetted against the sky. She looked so fragile. If she fell . . .

Amber gave herself a moment to focus, collect her thoughts. The narrow ledge that led to the laird's study was about four centimetres wide. Frankly, it didn't look inviting.

Li had given her instruction in free climbing and Amber had been quite good. Her years of horse-riding, windsurfing and water skiing had developed her balance and she was fit and strong. They had climbed along narrow ledges together – but of course they had been roped and Li had been there to correct her.

She couldn't think like that. She would have to imagine Li was with her, and they were climbing a slab of rock, not a building.

The stone windowsill was smooth beneath her feet. Actually, it wasn't too slippery – much less slippery than a slab of rock would have been. Good, she was calmer, noticing details. From that would come concentration. She flexed her toes and spread her arms along the golden stone wall. She checked her technique: hands close, elbows dropped, fingers well into the cracks.

She had started.

The wall was built of large blocks, so the first handhold was easy to find. She slid her foot along the small ledge, then pulled the other one after her. Li's voice in her head said: *Stick your bottom out.* The biggest mistake when climbing a slab was to hug the wall and flatten your body against it. Then your feet would slide off. Amber stuck her bottom out. Her weight went down through the balls of her feet and anchored her to the wall.

'*With perfect technique,*' Li had said many times, '*you can climb on hand- and footholds no wider than a coin.*'

Perfect technique. Li had perfect technique but Amber was still learning. When she moved, would she be able to keep the correct stance? She had an overwhelming urge to go back in through window.

But the others were depending on her. She had to go on.

Another of Li's phrases came back to her: '*Climbing is like meditation. One hand, then one foot, then the other hand, then the other foot. Small movements. If you make big movements you'll unbalance and fall. Small movements and you'll get there.*'

Amber found she had started to move towards the laird's window.

Down below she heard a noise, and someone whistling. She stopped dead still. A figure was walking down the alley below, swinging a black rubbish sack. Amber shrank away, trying not to be seen. Her feet started to slip and she stuck her bottom out again. Her heart rebounded against her ribs like a rubber ball.

Below, the kitchen worker opened the bin, tossed the rubbish bag in and headed back down the alleyway.

Amber took deep breaths. She moved on. She took it slowly, remembering Li's instructions. It would be so easy to rush, trying to stay out of sight. She kept her eyes on the pale brick, her fingers, sliding each foot one by one and letting it find its place. The rain started again but still she kept her slow rhythm.

At last the fingers of her right hand met the next window frame. Her toes touched the broad stone sill. Nearly there.

She moved her right hand so that her watch face tilted. In it she saw the reflection of the room. No one in there.

Amber grasped the window frame tightly and pulled herself onto the sill. It was so good to have proper handholds at last. The window was open just a crack. Amber slipped her fingers underneath and pushed up. It rose soundlessly. She slipped through and sprang down to the floor.

It was a wood-panelled room with a big stone fireplace. Quite cluttered, unlike the studied, artfully arranged grandeur of the rest of the lodge. This place looked lived in.

Clutter was good. It was easy to hide a bug in clutter. She took the bug out of her pocket. It was about the size of half an egg. She looked around. Now, where was the perfect hiding place?

Something caught her eye. It was a metal object, uncharacteristically industrial against the dark panelling: their metal detector. The gamekeepers must have brought it back. Well, that proved beyond doubt that the laird was involved.

There was a desk of dark wood with a red leather writing surface. She lifted the lid on a cigar box. Too obvious. Next to that was a miniature brass container like a coal scuttle. It held odds and ends – pens, scissors, a paintbrush. A good spot – but would the metal stop it transmitting?

A wickerwork bin stood by the desk. There were

papers in it – they would hide it nicely. She knelt down, put the bug inside it and flicked it on.

Then she heard something she didn't want to hear. Somebody was turning the doorknob.

24

THE INFORMATION

In the conference room next door, Hex heard the Bluetooth headphone spring into life. At first it was a jumble of sounds, like the kind of background noise you get when someone moves about on the phone. But then he began to make sense of it. And his spine went cold.

There were people moving about, feet on a carpet, somebody sitting down heavily in a chair. Voices all talking at once.

He ran to the window and peered out. He expected to see Amber making her way back, but the expanse of wall was empty. The only thing moving was the trees sagging as the rain came down. Amber was still in the room.

He listened for the sickening sound of a capture, but it didn't come. The group in the room were settling down for a meeting.

He had to focus, pay attention. This was the information Amber was risking her life to get.

'They're coming at ten.'

'But it's only just getting dark then.'

'It's raining. No one will be out walking. You won't be seen. Anyway, that's the time they want to come.'

'Aye. Let's get it shipped and out. This place has become too dangerous.'

'We should have got out before.'

A thump, like someone hitting a desk. 'I told Ivanovich we could deliver and we can. I'm not missing a big order like this and I'm not letting him down – he's got too many friends.' Hex wished he could see them. Was that the laird?

Hex picked up Amber's phone. He knew the others wouldn't be in range, but just in case something went wrong he texted them. '*Pickup 10pm. V jumpy B careful. Buyer name Ivanovich.*' He pressed SEND.

The voices carried on. 'We do the delivery. After that, we destroy it all. Go away. It's got too hot around here.'

They'd got the information. But where was Amber?

If they knew there was somebody in that room with them, what would they do?

Amber had her eye to the narrow strip of light. She could see figures moving about in the room. The laird was sitting at the big desk, his foot next to the bin where the bug was hidden. Two figures in tweeds paced the room, agitated – the gamekeepers.

She stood stock-still inside the cupboard. She hadn't had time to make it to the window and anyway she couldn't have got away in time. It was just luck that she'd noticed the panelled area on one end of the fireplace, where the panelling came out further than the chimney breast. It was a cupboard tall enough to stand in, and seemed to go back quite a long way so there was plenty of room. The air inside was stale and cold, the way a room smells if no one has been in it for weeks. A draught turned her wet clothes to ice, the stone floor froze her bare feet.

'They're coming to the factory at ten.'

Once the laird had said those words, she knew Hex would be texting the others. But there was something else they needed to know, something only she could see.

There were two more men – not dressed like the gamekeepers. They wore street clothes – dark T-shirts and dark baggy jeans. Amber couldn't see much of them through the crack but what she did see made her want to steer well clear of them. One was stocky, with broad shoulders, and his head was shaved. The other was bigger and fat, like a bouncer gone to seed. They had rough accents, not like the softer local accent of people who lived around here. One of them walked closer to the laird's desk to emphasize a point, and the way he moved would scare people in the toughest part of town.

The laird had brought in reinforcements to make sure the job went off without a hitch. Alex, Li and Paulo needed to be warned.

She heard the office door open, then slam. It must have been the gamekeepers leaving, because the heavies were still there and the laird still sat at the desk. He spread out a map and the heavies huddled close. Amber couldn't hear what they were saying, but it was obviously fairly involved. How long would they be? Amber couldn't wait for long – she had to warn the others.

Still the group huddled over the desk. They weren't looking in her direction. Could she creep out and escape?

No, she thought. It was far too risky. If they caught her she would be dead.

She felt behind her with her hands. The cupboard seemed to be quite deep – as if . . . She carefully took a step back. Her bare foot met stone. She took another step back. More stone. And another.

She was in a passage.

Amber turned round. Groping with her hands, she began to walk.

Exactly one hour after Alex had spoken to Hex, he arrived at the entrance for the next call. Behind him,

Paulo and Li stood shivering. It wasn't hard to be punctual when there was nothing else you had to do.

Hex's message bleeped through. Alex turned to the others. 'They've got it. Here, ten o'clock.'

'*Dios*,' breathed Paulo. 'I thought they'd never manage it.'

Alex quickly dialled Hex. 'Got it. Can you tip off the police safely?'

'No problem,' said Hex.

But Alex caught a note of caution in Hex's voice. He'd gone quiet, as if he was afraid of being heard.

'You OK, mate?'

'Yeah.' Hex's voice dropped to a whisper. 'A bunch of guys just went past, that's all. I'll call the police now. Somehow, I'm going to have to make them listen to me more seriously this time—'

'Collect Amber and get out. We'll see you when it's all over.' Alex cut the connection.

Li and Paulo jumped up. They looked animated again, purposeful. Alex felt his spirits rise as adrenaline kicked in. 'Let's get this show on the road.'

25

BORROWED TIME

Amber found herself at the bottom of a tight spiral staircase. Water dripped down, and high above was a tiny diamond window. She began to climb. Cobwebs brushed against her face. She tried not to think about the spiders who must be hitching a ride in her hair. The steps were gritty and wet under her bare feet. Up and up they went. Where would they come out? They couldn't have been built just to connect a cupboard in the laird's office with the roof, could they? One thing was for sure, with all these cobwebs, no one had been this way for a long time.

The triangular steps flattened out to form a small landing. A light showed in a narrow line. Another doorway?

She peered through the crack. An office of some sort, surrounded by shelves. A woman sat at a desk in the middle, a Glaickvullin Lodge name badge on her dark cardigan. Should she come out? What would the woman do? She might call hotel security.

Amber went on up and came to another landing with a wooden door. She listened and made out a voice: 'Honey, did you hear something?' American. Male.

There was a reply: 'Honey, you're always like this with jet lag. I said you should have stayed up.' Female. Also American. It was obviously someone's room.

Amber moved and stepped on a sharp piece of grit. She sucked her breath in through her teeth.

'What was that?' The man's voice sounded panicky. 'Is this place haunted?'

She seemed to have caught them off guard. If she had to escape through anywhere, a room with two jet-lagged guests was a better bet than a room with a member of staff.

Amber rapped on the panel smartly. 'Hello?' She pushed the panel open.

Staring at her was one of the American couples she had seen on the tour earlier. The man wore a navy blue eye mask pushed up on his forehead.

For once Amber was lost for words. She closed the cupboard door behind her and padded across the soft carpet to the double doors at the entrance to the suite.

'Hey – aren't you that pop star?' said the man.

Amber smiled. 'No, I just look like her.' She reached the door. 'Sleep well. Sorry to disturb you.'

Out on the landing she paused to get her bearings. A sign pointed to ROOMS 300–320, so she must be on the third floor. She had grey dust down both arms and her feet were gritty and filthy. Hex must be waiting for her down in the conference centre, but she couldn't go down there looking like this. Better go to their suite and call from there.

'Sounds good to me,' said Paulo. 'Do you think that will work?'

They were sitting in the tunnel, the plastic drainpipe snaking alongside them. Alex had a stick in his hand and they had been drawing diagrams in the mud as they worked out their plan.

Li nodded. 'They're terrified of fire in there. It's got one exit, it's enclosed. They could easily suffocate. They sent that guy outside when he wanted a cigarette.'

Alex prodded the plan he had drawn. 'We start a fire, the smoke brings them out, just in time for the police to see . . . Great, but what are we going to burn? We can't collect wood. Everything out there is sopping wet.'

Li shrugged her pack off her shoulders and opened it. 'We must have something in here that's dry.' She brought out a gas stove and weighed it in her hand. 'Too small?'

'That won't produce enough smoke,' said Paulo. He was rummaging in his pack too. 'Spare socks?'

'We're not trying to poison them,' said Li.

Alex sighed. 'It'll have to be the rope. But that will mean we've only got one possible exit.' He looked at the others. 'What do you think?'

They thought carefully. Li fingered the end of the rope, which was coiled diagonally across her body. 'I suppose we won't be needing it again . . .' Her voice trailed off. She wasn't a hundred per cent keen on burning a vital piece of equipment.

Paulo put his pack back on. 'The advantage of using the rope is that we can thread it into the crevice so that the smoke really gets in.' He shrugged. 'We've got to use it.'

'OK, agreed,' said Li. 'We burn the rope.'

Alex scrubbed out the diagram. He doubted whether anyone would ever find it, but it was standard practice to cover their tracks. 'Let's rehearse.'

Hex put the key to the conference room on the marble reception desk and then headed for the stairs. He was worried about Amber. He was going back to their suite and he hoped she'd be there. He put his foot on the bottom step.

A voice made him jump. 'How did you get in here? Are you dropping off the bikes or something?' Tiff.

She was coming down the stairs. Beside her was

the woman who had picked her up in the taxi earlier – her parents' PA. Both were dressed up for dinner.

'Hi, Tiff,' Hex had said, and tried to smile.

'Yeah, hello,' Tiff mumbled in her usual grudging way, and hurried away, explaining to the woman, 'He's one of the people from the hostel.'

The sooner I get out of here, thought Hex, the better. And I hope you choke on a canapé. Anyway, he had more pressing matters. He turned.

Someone was blocking his way. A figure with dark hair, a blue-green kilt, the rough army-style jumper replaced by an evening jacket and frilly shirt. The laird was standing above him on the stairs.

He gave Hex a courteous smile. 'Good to see you here. Was the hostel suitable for your needs?' The twang of London's East End was a reminder of the roughness beneath the smooth exterior.

Hex's mouth went dry. Was there any way to get away? 'The hostel was fine, thanks.' He looked at his watch. 'Listen, I'm late—'

The laird moved down a step so that he stood closer to Hex. Hex could see the black flecks in the brown eyes. 'I'm glad I caught you. There's something I need to ask you about the vehicles. Have you got a moment?'

Hex noticed two people close in behind him. He couldn't recall having seen them before. One was muscular, with a shaved head. The other was big and fleshy. They closed in and forced him to turn round and go down the stairs again. They herded him through the hall and down the narrow passageway. The laird turned to the other men and fiddled with his cufflinks. 'If you just carry on, there's something I have to do.' He moved away.

Now Hex was alone with the two men.

His phone rang. The bald guy snatched it from Hex's waistband and his heart started hammering. Who was it?

The man lifted it to his ear, the blue glow of the screen illuminating the side of his head. 'Who is this?'

Hex kept his face impassive. Inside he was repeating, *Hang up now, don't say anything.*

The man took the phone away from his ear and put it in his pocket. Whoever it was had hung up – but at least somebody now knew he was in trouble.

They walked out through the back door and into the big yard. The rain had stopped now and the bustle had died down. The birds had been fed, the tools tidied away. Music wafted over from the dining room. A ceilidh was starting up: plenty of noise to cover whatever the men planned to do with him, Hex thought.

Tiff came out of the dining room, hand in hand with a tall blond-haired lad. 'Let's go somewhere quiet,' she said. 'There are too many people in there.'

'How about down here?' said the boy. Bagpipes started playing a reel and he whirled Tiff around in a circle and pulled her into the dark corridor.

Tiff hefted up her long skirt and tried to keep up, her arm outstretched. 'No, that goes out to the farmyard,' she laughed. 'It's the smelly bit.'

The boy turned to her, eyes glinting wickedly. 'But it's quiet.'

She could see some men in the yard. They weren't dressed in the normal farm stuff she had seen before. They were standing in front of an open door.

The boy saw them and turned to Tiff. 'Too crowded. Let's find somewhere else.'

Something made Tiff look back and saw that one of the figures was Hex. A large man threw him into the storeroom, hard, as though he was trying to hurt him. The other man raised a gun, pointed it into the storeroom and fired. Tiff gave a cry and jumped.

The boy put an arm across her shoulders and tried to pull her towards the main hall. 'It's people hunting. An adventuring tigress like you isn't scared of gunshots, is she?'

Tiff wrestled free and looked back. The two men stood at the door to the storeroom. The one with the gun was still firing. Fear rose in her throat: there was something about the way he did it, clinically, coldly. Six shots, one after the other.

26

THE TRAP

The air was filled with the scream of jet engines. Li looked up the crevice. Five fighter planes cut through the air like black arrows and roared away into the distance. As the sound faded they heard something else: a vehicle engine being cut.

Li, Paulo and Alex were in position in the tunnel where the ventilation pipe went into the factory.

Paulo only needed a second to identify the vehicle. 'A Range Rover,' he said quietly.

Li, poised further up in the crack in the rock, could just about see out. 'It's them.'

The two gamekeepers slammed the vehicle doors. A big man with a hood pulled up over his head got out more slowly, taking his time. Ivanovich. The evening sun glinted off the piercings in his nose, his bottom lip, his cheek. Li couldn't forget a face like that.

One of the gamekeepers felt in his pocket and walked towards Li. She could see the lacings on his boots. He was barely three metres away. Silent as a cat, she stepped down in case he could see her – although he shouldn't be able to. The three friends had smeared mud all over themselves and were well camouflaged.

The gamekeeper took a small device out of his pocket and pointed it at the ground. It let out a high-pitched beep. Deep in the metal structure they felt rather than heard something moving. The trapdoor must have an electronic lock. They hadn't heard it before because they hadn't been that close.

Good job we didn't try going in there, thought Paulo. We'd never have got past something like that.

They heard the trapdoor open. Footsteps rang on the metal rungs, resonated on the walls of the container and shuddered down the plastic pipe. They heard him step off at the bottom. Light sliced through the crevice as he flashed his torch around. His footsteps came towards them.

The three friends tried to shrink into the shadows. What if he saw the trail of blue climber's rope that snaked along the crack beside the pipe?

There was a noise like an engine turning over. Then it started running. The generator was on.

Alex grasped Paulo's and Li's hands and gave them a squeeze. The countdown had started.

Alex took his survival kit out of his pocket and took the lid off. He removed a small pack of matches, wrapped in cling film. Just as they'd rehearsed, Li put out her hand and took the rest of the kit.

The walls resonated as the other two figures climbed down the ladder. Got them, thought Alex. They were ready to do their bit. Would the police be in time?

The air was starting to roar again. The fighter jets were coming back. To Paulo, something about the noise was a little bit different. They swooped away and circled back.

Definitely different. Under the cry of the jets was a beating, a rhythm. A helicopter. The police were here. They'd used the jets as cover.

Alex struck a match and it flared, then went out. Li held the tin so he could try again. He struck another. It flared, then died.

Paulo looked up. The planes were criss-crossing the sky, banking and turning. Hopefully the men couldn't hear it in the factory, especially with the noise of the generator, but the cover wouldn't last for ever.

Alex discarded a third match. He sighed with frustration and moved a dead squirrel out of the way with his foot so he could get closer to the rope.

'Are they wet?' whispered Li.

'They're waterproof,' hissed Alex. 'They'll light no matter what. You've seen them.'

Paulo looked up again. Li suddenly felt faint. A cough welled up in her throat and she pressed her mouth together in a tight line. If she coughed it would give their position away.

Alex was on his fourth match. The same thing happened. What was going on? He looked at the dead match in his hand, puzzled. Overhead the jets screamed. The noise seemed to throb in his head and he let it fall forwards against the drainpipe.

Paulo didn't feel too good either. His foot touched a dead vole and he felt sick. He tilted his head back to take a breath of fresh air from the crevice.

Fresh air . . . He suddenly realized. There must be a backdraught, washing the fumes from the generator back down into the cave. That was why the matches wouldn't light. The cave was filling with carbon monoxide and putting them out. That's why there were all these dead creatures. It was like being locked in a small garage with the car engine running. If they didn't get out, they would asphyxiate too.

Alex suddenly found himself snapping awake, as though he had been about to fall asleep. Paulo was shaking him and pointing up the passageway.

Alex was confused but his training took over. If Paulo thought something was dangerous enough to abort a mission, he didn't argue. He crawled.

Li was slumped against the wall, her head moving slowly from side to side. Paulo threaded his arm under her shoulders. She lay across him as though she was drowning. With the other arm, he pulled himself along after Alex.

Hex stared at the man as the sixth bullet emptied into the blue drum near his feet. The bald man didn't say a word, just concentrated on shooting. A professional.

Finished, he slammed the door. Hex heard the lock click.

The room became dark, except for a small window above the door. Too small to escape through, it was more like a large glass letterbox than a window.

The drums started to leak. The fumes caught his throat; it squeezed tight and he coughed violently. Through watering eyes he tried to read the label: PMK. He didn't know what that was, but it had a big orange label with a cross on it, and underneath the word 'HARMFUL'. He coughed again. Other labels came into focus. METHYLAMINE. That accounted for the smell – amines, if chemistry lessons were to be believed, smelled sharp and fishy. Next to methylamine was a row of orange labels. HIGHLY FLAMMABLE. HARMFUL. CORROSIVE. A box at the back labelled KETAMINE.

He tried to climb up on the drums but they slithered down in a slippery avalanche. Hex stepped out of the way and looked around the walls. Was there an air brick, a ventilation hole of some sort? No, nothing. He coughed again and kicked a drum out of the way. Why were there so many? If you needed that much chemical, wouldn't a big one be easier?

Give his brain a problem, he would try to solve it. There were a lot of small drums because you could hide them in a deer carcass. Just like he'd seen the previous night when he and Li were watching the gamekeepers. That way you could take raw materials up to the factory on the moor without being seen.

For a moment Hex felt quite proud of himself for the deduction. Then a spasm seized his throat. It was more than coughing; it was retching.

There must be a way out – but the walls were smooth and solid. Only one way in and out. One tiny window and no way to break it. The perfect place to keep a stack of illicit chemicals and the perfect place to keep an inconvenient guest out of sight. No difficult bullet holes for a coroner to query. They could just leave him in here with this noxious stuff until he was done, then remove him to some desolate spot and no one would know what had happened. He could disappear as efficiently as they undoubtedly would.

His eyes were streaming. The foul-smelling liquid was forming pools on the bare concrete floor; soaking into the cardboard ketamine box. Tears were streaming down his face. His nose and throat were raw. He kept retching in dry heaves.

Hex had really thought he was going to die when the man got out the gun. When the bullets went into the blue drums of chemicals, he had actually felt relieved. Now that seemed rather naïve. Perhaps it might have been better if they had just shot him.

27

LAST CHANCE

Alex crawled fast. Above, the sound of the helicopter and the fighter planes dwindled away. Were they leaving? Or was it just that he couldn't hear them any more? Was that also their hopes of flushing these guys out?

They crawled past the end of the exhaust pipe. Behind him, Li had revived. Paulo brought up the rear, pushing them on.

When they reached the end of the tunnel, Paulo stopped and they all gulped in fresh air. For a minute they all lay there, gasping.

Alex looked back the way they had come. 'We've got to get back. The police are waiting.'

Paulo pulled him back. '*Hombre*, we can't. We'll die. And you'll never get the rope lit because there's no oxygen for it to burn.'

Li looked rather sick. She pushed some rocks out of the way and sat with her back against the tunnel wall. Paulo checked her pulse. 'I'm still alive,' she muttered, but she sounded faint. Perhaps because she was the smallest she had been worst affected.

Paulo moved away and winced as he bent his finger back on one of the pieces of rock she had moved. As he sucked the wound he had an idea. 'Pick up some of these,' he said, and grabbed a couple of small rocks.

Alex watched him crawl at top speed back down the tunnel, one-handed. He scooped up some rocks and followed.

Paulo had stopped at the end of the pipe. The smell of diesel fumes made Alex feel sick. Paulo was stuffing the pieces of rock into the end of the pipe. Alex passed him his. They fitted in nicely.

After a few seconds Alex could have sworn the

tang of diesel fumes was less strong. Paulo sat back on his haunches and grinned. 'In about sixty seconds they will smell fumes in there and the generator will stop. At that point the rats will come swarming out of their lair.'

They hurried back to Li. She was still taking deep breaths but was looking more alert.

Paulo ran his torch over her. 'How do you feel?'

'A bit sick,' Li said. 'I'll be fine.'

She got to her feet and staggered a little. Alex put out his arm and she took it. He realized he could still hear the planes.

Paulo took Li's other arm. 'Come on, let's go and see the show.'

The tunnel led upwards to a dusky sky. With every step they took towards the light the air became cooler and fresher. The sound of the planes and the helicopter became louder. The last part sloped up steeply.

Cautiously, the three members of Alpha Force emerged.

Up on the hill, the trapdoor was open, its light shining into the sky. A helicopter skimmed ten metres off the ground, a triangle of light trailing from it like a skirt. Figures were running around on the moor. The skirt of light touched them, then lost them, then found them again. A shot was fired. Another helicopter circled in the sky, its spotlight brushing over a number of bulky figures, crouched over sniper rifles around the moor. Armed police.

If the police hadn't believed them before, they certainly did now.

The gamekeepers were heading down the hill towards them. A pistol cracked. The submachine guns answered. Further off in the darkness Li saw a hooded shape, piercings twinkling, moving away in the darkness.

'Ivanovich,' she hissed. A wave of giddiness passed over her and she lay back against the opening of the cave.

Paulo saw the drug dealer. A bulky figure was moving about ten metres away in the heather – a police marksman. But he was facing the wrong way. He hadn't seen Ivanovich.

They couldn't shout for his attention. They'd never be heard in all the confusion.

Paulo squirmed forwards on his belly and tapped the rifleman on the shoulder. A head snapped round. Eyes looked at him from behind a balaclava. Paulo pointed at Ivanovich, half running, half crawling down the steep hill. The sniper fired, and the night lit up with starbursts of muzzle flash as other hidden gunmen followed his lead, the sound swallowed by the beat of the helicopter.

The heli passed overhead, its spotlight swinging and illuminating Paulo. He was on an open patch of ground. Alerting the sniper had stopped Ivanovich getting away, but it had put him right in the line of fire.

He needed to get back under cover. He began to crawl, elbows digging into the earth.

The spotlight swung away. Alex saw that the gamekeepers were facing a line of armed police, bulked out by body armour. They raised their hands in surrender. Paulo was crawling towards him, his eyes glinting with determination.

The heli found Ivanovich and its spotlight picked him out, his gun raised, defiant. He fired.

Paulo felt something hit him, hard like a punch.

His ears rang and something warm spread over his arm.

Alex saw Paulo falter, an arm outstretched. He grabbed it and pulled his friend the rest of the way to cover. The spotlight slid over them as Alex dragged Paulo into the cave mouth. He had something wet and dark all over him and his face was rigid with pain, his arm dark and wet.

Down below them, Ivanovich lifted his pistol but the trigger produced only a click. He was out of bullets. Two policemen grabbed him from behind and shook the gun out of his hand.

The fighter planes were coming back. They zigzagged across the sky as if in a salute and took off into the wide blue yonder.

Li and Alex yelled at the top of their lungs: 'Man down!'

28

PRISONER

Crash! Hex looked up with bleary eyes. The window had just been broken.

He jumped to his feet. The rubber soles of his shoes made sticky noises in the chemical lake on the floor. The leaking drums slid away as he tried to climb on them, but he wasn't going to give up. He dragged the ketamine box over, climbed on it and gulped in the fresh air like a drowning man.

The cold made his inflamed nose and eyes stream even more, but it was bliss.

'Hex!'

He blinked away tears and saw a small blonde figure in the yard looking up at him, a flash of glitter in her hair.

It was the last person he had expected. Tiff.

'Hex, are you all right?'

Hex nodded.

'Did they shoot you?'

Hex shook his head. He was too busy breathing to talk.

'I saw them.' Her voice was high and upset. 'I saw them throw you in here and shoot you.'

Hex tried to tell her to be quiet, but his voice wouldn't work. What if the men were still around? Or the laird? They couldn't fail to hear her yelling in the middle of the yard. She was putting herself in danger.

On the second attempt he managed a loud croak. 'Tiff, shhh.'

She didn't hear him. 'I thought they'd killed you—'

Hex managed a shout. 'Tiff, shut up!'

She looked up, offended. The light caught on the glitter in her hair. It was a hair slide.

'Sorry,' said Hex. He'd better grovel: she was his only chance. 'Tiff, I'm really pleased to see you. Can you help me get out? Give me that hair clip.'

A look of suspicion flitted over her face. Had he blown it?

'Tiff, please. I need to pick the lock.'

Still looking at him suspiciously, her hands went up to her hair.

Then Hex noticed two figures behind her in the semi-darkness. 'Run, Tiff!' he yelled. 'Run!'

She started to look annoyed. The bouncer grabbed her from behind and lifted her off the ground. She kicked and screamed, but her kicks and blows hit empty air. He clamped a hand over her mouth and cut off her screams.

Hex watched, horrified. The bald man came out. In the yard the indicators of a Range Rover came alive and he opened the back door. Hex recognized it. It was the Range Rover they'd rented.

The big man bundled Tiff into the vehicle. His hand slipped down from her mouth and she let out a full-throated yell – 'Hex! Help! Help me!'

The bald man came to the storeroom door, a

revolver in his hand. Hex leaped down from the window, plunging into the acrid sea of fumes. He doubled over, unable to control the coughing, helpless as the door was unlocked.

Hex saw the man reel back when the smell hit him. *Go!* he thought. He lunged forwards while the guy was off balance, knocked him over and the gun spun away. He tried to hold him down as he reached for it, but the man squirmed and bucked.

A scream brought everyone to a standstill.

'Hex!' Tiff.

The big man had Tiff pinned down on the back seat of the Range Rover, her right arm twisted up behind her back.

'Are you going to come quietly,' he said, 'or does your girlfriend have to die?'

Tiff let out a sob.

Hex had no choice. He couldn't save Tiff *and* himself. She shouldn't even be mixed up in this. He relaxed his hold.

The bald man retrieved his gun. He got to his feet and nudged Hex in the back, pushing him towards the Range Rover. 'Move.'

Reluctantly, Hex climbed into the vehicle. The man got in beside him.

The big man set the child locks. There goes any chance of opening the doors while we're moving, thought Hex.

The engine started, the accelerator gunned and the Range Rover swung out into the road.

The sky was a pinkish colour; the sun was starting to go down. Hex could see the clock in the dashboard: ten to ten. The others should have captured the gamekeepers by now. Had they? Did these guys know? If they did, there would be hell to pay.

If the others had failed . . . That wasn't worth even thinking about.

Tiff huddled close to him. He had never seen her so scared. The vehicle was so familiar; they had been in it most days for the past few weeks. Now a man sat beside him, watching them with a gun. It felt like their home had been invaded.

The bald man nudged Hex with the gun. Hex turned to look at him. He was holding out his hand. On it were four white pills.

'Take two and give the other two to her.'

The gun barrel reminded Hex that he had no choice. He picked up the pills. Tiff looked at him with fearful eyes.

'What are they?' Hex asked.

'Special K,' said the driver.

Special K. Ket. Vitamin K. Ketamine. Veterinary anaesthetic.

The bald man's eyes narrowed. He twitched the end of his gun. 'Go on. It'll hurt less.'

Hex felt Tiff's fingernails curl into his arm.

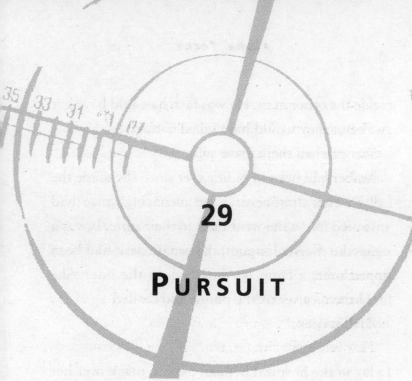

29

PURSUIT

A hooded figure got up from the narrow window seat in the morning room. Amber had covered her dirty tweeds with a floor-length velvet cape from the restaurant cloakroom. With her black skin it had made her invisible to anyone who glanced into the darkened window.

She had seen everything in the yard. She saw Tiff throw the brick through the window. She saw her yelling at Hex. She saw the big man seize her. She saw brave Hex explode out of the storeroom and tackle the other man. He was fast; he could have got away. But they would have killed Tiff.

She watched them drive away.

Amber had been in hiding ever since she made the call to Hex's phone and the menacing voice had answered. Now she went back to their suite. It was a mess: the chaises longues, the ornate desk had been tipped over; a lamp lay smashed on the floor. She lifted the receiver of the phone and dialled.

'Hello, Alex?'

Li lay in the hospital bed, an oxygen mask over her face. She knew Paulo was in a room somewhere near, having tests, but the last she had seen was when the medics got them into the helicopter. Medics had put oxygen masks on her and Alex, and crowded around Paulo. She could only see their backs, watch their urgent movements, see stethoscopes, tubes, needles and bloodstained pads. Their mouths were moving but the whine of the heli drowned out their words. The mask felt like it was suffocating her. She pulled it off and a police officer gently replaced it again. In the moment before it enclosed her nose and mouth she caught a faint smell. Charred flesh.

When they had touched down at the hospital, a team of medics swooped on each of them and swept her away to examine her. She wasn't able to see either Paulo or Alex.

The doctors had done co-ordination tests on her and said she had some neurological damage from inhaling carbon monoxide. She kept taking off her oxygen mask and demanding to know about her friends. They were being taken care of, she was told, and the mask would be gently replaced. But Paulo was shot, she had said. He's being taken care of, she was told and the mask was patiently replaced again.

After a few hours of rest and concentrated oxygen therapy she should be all right, they said. But staying calm and quiet was driving Li mad.

She was in a small ward. Her agitated brain had taken in every inch of the room: the tiny floral pattern on the curtained screens, presumably to make them look more homely than clinical; the clock radio glowing on the bedside table; the dim light in the corridor. If she wasn't attached to this oxygen tank, she'd be wandering around the corridors, looking for the others.

Someone came in. She recognized Alex's step before he pulled back the curtain. She sat bolt upright and pulled her mask off. 'They've let you out! Why aren't you on one of these?'

He sat on the bed. 'I think I was lucky. There's more of me, I suppose.' He still had smears of mud all over his face and clothes, like camouflage cream.

'How's Paulo?'

'They're still doing tests.' He took Hex's palmtop out of his pocket. 'Amber called. There were two other guys working with the drug guys. They've got Hex.' He showed her the palmtop screen. On it was Hex's tracer, moving into the hills.

Li swallowed. 'Oh my God.'

Alex put the palmtop back in his pocket and got up. 'Is your phone still working?'

'Yes.'

Alex was moving backwards, heading for the door. 'Keep it on standby in case I need to contact you. I've told the police and given them the registration of our old Range Rover. Amber said that's what they're using. I'll see you later.'

Li reached down and hooked her phone out of the bedside cabinet. Its screen glowed as she switched it on. 'Are you sure you should go? The police have loads of guys out.'

But Alex knew it was a rhetorical question. When one of your friends is in enemy hands, you need as many rescuers as possible, to cover all the angles. You don't leave it to someone else while you've got breath in your body.

'I wish I could come with you,' said Li.

He waved and disappeared.

Paulo was lying on a treatment table. Two men in white coats stood with their backs to him examining a set of x-rays. He could see the glowing monochrome shadows of his bones but they gave nothing away.

At first it hadn't hurt; perhaps because he hadn't fully realized what had happened. He'd even carried on crawling, which surprised him. He thought that if you'd been shot, you'd be knocked over, like you would if you'd been hit by a car. He even had time to think about it a bit. Of course, it made sense. If the force of the bullet was enough to knock him over, it would also knock over the person who fired the gun.

That was the last coherent thought he had.

The doctors had given him morphine, but the pain was like nothing he'd ever experienced before. He'd had injuries before. If you handled big, strong animals all the time you got used to being knocked about. But sprains and broken bones were nothing compared with this. It was a sickening pain, searing through his shoulder like a red-hot lance. He imagined the track of the bullet, the flesh it had torn through. He could smell his own flesh charring. It was truly brutal, like burning off a part of your body.

'I can't see a bullet in there,' said one doctor.

'Let's see what the arteriogram says,' said the other. He turned to Paulo. 'Good news, it looks like it's gone right through.'

Paulo's stomach turned. He never thought he would be so upset by a wound. Maybe the morphine would kick in soon.

* * *

Alex left the hospital. The police had wasted no time in setting off. The helicopter was lifting into the sky, lights winking as it swooped over his head. Sirens were sounding and tyres were scrambling on gravel as unmarked Land Rovers headed for the hills. Glaickvullin community hospital had probably never seen so much action.

On the moor behind the hospital, a pair of headlights was joggling over the bumpy ground. They came down into the floodlit hospital car park. A quad bike, a slender black figure at the handlebars.

Amber braked and slid to a stop beside Alex. 'You look rough.' She spoke briskly.

Alex climbed on. 'Where did you get this?'

'It's still ours technically. I reclaimed it and hotwired it again. Where's Hex?'

Alex showed her the palmtop.

Amber glanced at it, then turned to face forwards again. 'Right. Hold on tight.'

30

KETAMINE

Hex kept looking at his watch. He didn't know how long it took for the drug to start working, but it must have been about twenty minutes since he had taken it. He'd tried to palm the tablets, but the man insisted on seeing them on his tongue. He'd tried to spit them out but they'd dissolved instantly. There was no escape.

Tiff slumped beside him, silent. Her eyes were two grim slits, as if she was concentrating fiercely on resisting the drug. She had good reason to dread it. Hex kept remembering what Alex had looked like after he'd taken some, when it was mixed with something else. The terror on his face, the panic.

They'd had two whole tablets each. Undiluted.

How did it start? An itch on his arm – was that normal? His burning throat and nostrils – were they that bad before? Was the road really this bumpy?

Tiff suddenly seemed to grow taller in the seat. She sat up very straight and grabbed him. She looked into his eyes with wide black pupils. 'Slow down!' she shouted.

They weren't going that fast, but the fear in her voice was genuine.

The bald man spoke to her sharply. 'Be quiet.'

Hex patted her hand in an attempt to reassure her. But now he felt something too. And he didn't like it.

It felt like the vehicle was speeding downhill, out of control.

Tiff dug her hands into his skin like claws. 'Help me,' she whispered.

Help her? He was in a bad enough state himself. He tried the door. The handle moved freely but didn't engage. He saw himself in the window, a hollow-eyed face against the gloom, fighting to get out.

'Child lock,' the bald man reminded him.

Hex saw the speedo. It said 70 kph. If he left the car at that speed he'd be killed. A thought occurred to him and he smiled sardonically. Well, at least it might not hurt.

Tiff collapsed against his shoulder. She tried to move her arm but it just twitched. She was losing control of her limbs. Of course. She was much lighter than him. Two tablets would be bound to affect her faster than him.

The vehicle stopped. Hex breathed a prayer. Thank goodness.

There was a clunk as the door was opened from the outside. Hex jumped.

'Get out.' The bald man pushed him roughly and levelled the pistol at him.

Hex tried to obey, but Tiff was like a dead weight. Even a fragile-looking thing like her was amazingly heavy when she had no muscular control. He had to grab the door frame to lever himself out.

The fresh air hit him and caught in his throat. He tried to stand but his limbs felt very alien. He didn't dare let go of the side of the Range Rover.

'Get her out,' said the big man.

Hex turned and tried to comply, but could only cling to the door. The bald man got out of the other side and pulled her across by the shoulders. Her heels dragged two marks in the velour of the back seat; her eyes stared at Hex.

Hex became aware of a sound. The sea. Waves, brushing up against sand and pebbles. Under his feet was shingle. They were on the beach. What did this mean? What were the men going to do?

On the other side of the Range Rover, the man let go of Tiff. She flopped to the ground and made a noise as if she had been winded. The bald man shone his torch on her and her eyes looked back, big and black. She tried to avoid the light but couldn't. Hex felt a wave of anger. She didn't deserve to end up like this: dying a frightening death at the hands of vicious drug traffickers.

'We can come back for her,' said the big man. He grabbed Hex under one arm. The bald man took him under the other arm and the gun brushed against Hex's cheek. As if he could do anything: he couldn't even walk. The men hoisted him along and he tried to move his legs but they wouldn't work.

His legs started to grow, then shrink. He looked down: he couldn't see them, but he could feel them. His legs were growing and twisting, the bones were changing, shrivelling. On his right the bald man said something to him but Hex didn't hear. He only saw a distorted mouth with an extra row of teeth, a bald skull rippling like melting plastic. Hex cried out and tried to retreat but the men held him firmly.

Ahead was a black shape in the cliff. A hole full of terror and blackness, like a bad dream. Hex shrank away and struggled, trying to crawl backwards away from the black thing; but he was carried in through its maw.

The rock underneath gave way to soft sand. It sucked at his feet. His legs were being eaten away. He gave a whimper but the men forced him further into the sand. His head scraped on the roof of the cave. He couldn't pull it out of the way but it didn't hurt.

The men dropped him and he lay there like a discarded rag. They went away. Hex watched their lights disappear, leaving him in total darkness. He tried to move but all he could do was hear and smell. The cave smelled of salt water, and an acrid, searing chemical. Methylamine.

The torches came back. The men were dragging Tiff along. They took her past him and dropped her. He heard a splash.

They came back for him, hoisted him up and within moments he was plummeting down a hole in the floor of the cave. He hit the water and went under, but then came up again. A torch picked out Tiff next to him, floating helplessly, like a carcass.

Alex clutched the palmtop in one hand, and held on for dear life with the other. Amber was throwing the bike across the dark ground. She stopped for nothing, just rode all the bumps as if they were the fences at the Grand National. Police helicopters wheeled in the distance, red and white lights winking in time with the beat of their rotors.

Something changed on the lighted display. Alex checked it, then tapped Amber on the shoulder.

She braked and Alex nearly tumbled off. He

caught himself, then gasped, 'Hex's trace has gone.' He showed her the map. 'Here. On the coast.'

She nodded, then gunned the throttle. If she had been driving with grim determination before, she pushed the bike even harder now. Alex tucked the palmtop into his pocket and held on tight.

There were two situations in which the tracers didn't show. Underground and underwater. Losing contact like that meant Hex must be in even greater danger.

For a while Hex began to think the men had just left them there in the water-filled shaft. He tried to move again, tried to get out. From what he'd seen in the torchlight, it would be simple – the water level was less than half a metre from the lip of the shaft. He could just haul himself out, then get Tiff. But his arms and legs felt like they had disappeared.

He kept telling himself that was just an effect of the drug, a hallucination. Thank God he had seen Alex in this state too. Alex hadn't known what was happening to him, but thanks to him, Hex did. He clung to that knowledge.

He called out, 'Tiff?'

A blurred sort of cry was his answer. That at least was reassuring. Her head must be above water for her to be able to make a noise.

But for how long? And how long would he last?

There were other times in his life when he'd been trapped underground. Whenever he went underground, there seemed to be a fifty-fifty chance that something awful would happen.

'Hey, Tiff,' he said. 'You were right. Potholing sucks.'

There was no answer.

'Tiff? Tiff, talk to me.'

Another painful noise. It was all she could produce.

This drug really did give a horrible sensation. He couldn't move, but he knew what was going on. He would be aware of every moment before he died.

Then his super-sensitive hearing picked up another sound. The men were coming back.

31

THE CAVE

The breeze brought a scent of salt. They must be very near the coast. Amber saw the lighted area of ground in front of her dip away. She weighed it up. The surface was rocky, but the quad's tyres could cope. She threw it down the slope and leaned back.

Alex lay back too. He bounced in the seat, his knuckles smashing against the metal housing underneath it.

At last they levelled out. Amber braked and cut the engine. Far off they heard the beat of a helicopter.

Alex shone his torch on the ground. He was hoping to see tyre tracks, but the beach was pebbly. He checked the palmtop. They had come out almost to where the Kyle met the sea. He looked up and, in the distance, back towards the land, the bridge crossing the Kyle showed up like a dark bar against the moonlit clouds.

Alex's torch picked out a shape. He grabbed Amber's arm. 'They're still here.'

As Amber's eyes adjusted she recognized it. The Range Rover.

They hopped off the quad and hunkered down in the shadows. It wasn't much cover but it was better than nothing. Alex dialled the police, mentally thanking Hex for setting it up as a satellite phone.

The palmtop gave two bleeps and the screen light went out. Amber swore. 'It's out of batteries.'

'That's all we need,' sighed Alex. 'Of course, it would have been too convenient to be able to whistle up a heli.'

A sound made them catch their breath. Alex slipped the palmtop into his pocket and they listened, ready to flee.

But the noise wasn't someone approaching. It was blows.

Amber looked around wildly. 'Where's it coming from?'

'I don't know.' Alex's mind worked rapidly, trying to work out what it was. A brutal sound, again and again. It made him think of wood being chopped; films he'd seen of seals being bludgeoned. But where was it coming from?

Amber looked right and left and ran to the Range Rover. She crouched in its shadow and flashed her torch around. But the only thing she saw was the sea and the dark rock wall.

Alex ran over to join her. Still the sound continued – dull thud after dull thud coming out of the darkness like a sinister machine. But where was it?

Then they saw a flash of light on the shore, a little way away from the vehicle. It flickered and then disappeared.

'They're in a cave,' said Amber.

The sickening noise came again. What were they doing to Hex?

Alex felt fury rise in his throat like bile. 'Right, we

do the car,' he said. 'They can't get away if it doesn't have tyres.' He went to the front wheel.

Amber grabbed him. 'Then that leaves them stranded here with us.'

Alex pulled away from her and squatted down.

Amber went round in front of him and took him by the shoulders. 'Listen. I've seen those men, they've got guns, they're vicious. If we let them get away we can help Hex – if we're not too late . . . If they're stuck here they'll turn on us. Our only hope of helping Hex is if we stay alive.'

The sound stopped and a torch flashed around the beach.

Amber and Alex shrank back into the shadows. The men were coming back to the Range Rover. The noise of the helicopter circled close and then moved away.

'We'll go without lights,' said one of the men. 'That way they won't find us.'

They climbed in and started the engine. The tyres spun on the pebbles, then found a grip. The four-wheel drive roared, then took them up onto the moor and away.

Alex and Amber wasted no time. Keeping low, they ran from their hiding place to the area where they had seen the men. Yes, it was a cave.

Amber flashed her torch in. 'Hex?' she called. 'Hex! Tiff!'

The sound echoed back at her.

'Hex!' called Alex.

Trembling, Amber stepped into the cave. There were rocks scattered all over the floor. 'Hex! Tiff!'

The only answer was dripping water. Were they too late? Would they find Hex and Tiff beaten to death?

Amber walked towards the back of the cave. The floor became sandy, swallowing her boots. She went slowly, shining her torch in front of her feet. Then she found the shaft.

She shone her torch in. It glanced off something blue. A jumble of blue drums. 'Alex!' she called.

Alex picked his way over to her. The shaft was filled with chemical drums. A pair of eyes looked up from them, the nose barely above the water line.

'Tiff!' exclaimed Alex.

Tiff stared at him blankly. Was she alive?

Alex put his torch down on the edge of the shaft and reached for her. Tiff remained where she was, staring, silent, her expression unchanging.

'Amber, I think they're drugged. They can't move.'

Alex slipped into the water. It was full of drums. His feet touched them and they turned round like slippery balls. He tried to push the surface ones aside but they hardly moved. They must have been weighed down with stones to stop them floating out if the shaft flooded to the top.

At least that explained what the noise was. It was the men throwing them in. They must have drugged Hex and Tiff, then dumped these barrels on top of them so that they would drown.

He reached Tiff and tilted her head back. She was breathing very shallowly. Right. Now he just had to get her out.

'Hex!' called Amber. She was searching every shadow between the drums, going over and over them, she still hadn't found him. Finally she spotted a pale patch.

Like Tiff, only his eyes and nose were poking out. He was nearly under the water.

Amber left her torch on the edge and slipped in.

'Watch these drums,' called Alex. With one arm he held Tiff under her shoulders. With the other he tried to push drums out of the way. His feet slipped and he thudded down on the drums.

Amber half walked, half waded through them. Her feet slipped from under her and she carried on on all fours. Hex looked at her. His eyes were open, but nothing moved. A barrel rolled under her shoulder and she crashed into the water on her side. It tasted sharp, tainted with the chemicals that had washed out of the barrels. She emerged, spitting. The cave resonated with hollow booms as Alex tried to fight his way out with Tiff.

Amber went the rest of the way sliding on her belly. She reached Hex. His dark eyes seemed alert but expressionless. She tilted his head back so that the mouth was uncovered but he didn't move. He was helpless. 'OK,' she muttered to herself. 'How are we going to get you out?'

She slipped down in the water and tried to pull at his shoulders. His short dark hair against her face smelled pungently chemical. She pulled again and he came up a little, but this wasn't going to be easy. He was strong and fit, and all that muscle made for a lot of weight.

Alex reached the edge of the shaft and pulled Tiff out. Her face looked up, lifeless. He put his ear down to her nose and mouth. She wasn't breathing any more.

Alex opened her mouth and checked. Her airway was clear. He took a deep breath, pinched her nose and tilted her head back for the kiss of life.

Amber pulled on Hex's shoulders again, but still he wouldn't move. She braced her feet on a drum and gave a good yank, but he was stuck. The drums rolled under her feet and she went crashing under him.

Amber kicked out to push herself up. The drum she had her feet on revolved and she slipped further down. That seemed to free Hex. He rolled, his broad back solid on top of her. She pushed up but there was nothing to spring off, just those rotating barrels. She flailed with her hands but the body was still on top of her. She opened her eyes – she could see nothing and they stung with the tainted water. Her lungs were bursting. Her clawing hands met only Hex's unresponsive skin and more of those barrels.

Hex thought he had entered hell. He knew Amber was stuck underneath him but he couldn't move to free her. If he hadn't been drugged, he could have rolled or got out of the way. He could have called to Alex, who was kneeling over Tiff, concentrating on getting her to breathe.

Hex couldn't feel Amber, but he could hear her. He could hear the muffled sounds of her fists and legs pummelling on the barrels, as they uselessly rotated like ball bearings. She was slipping further in like a stick into quicksand.

The drumming was getting fainter. How long had she been under? If only he could move.

His confused brain gave him a reboot. Remember when you saw Alex on the drug. This might be another hallucination. His logical brain was trying to defend him, trying to keep him sane. He couldn't really be about to kill Amber. It must be something from his worst claustrophobic nightmare. She wasn't really going to die here, in this cave, trapped by his useless body.

Another voice sounded in his ear. 'Come on, you useless lump.'

Alex. He heaved at Hex's arm. Hex bumped over the barrels like rollers on a conveyor belt. Beyond him he heard Amber explode to the surface.

Alex looked up into the sky. The helicopter beat through the air, circling. He tucked the waterproof matches back into his survival tin and put it in his pocket. A branch stood upright in the pebble beach, the top a plume of flame. With petrol from the quad bike and a T-shirt, Alex had made a distress signal.

Amber was paddling in the sea, washing the chemical tainted water off her skin. Tiff and Hex were lying on the pebbles, breathing in the cool night air.

The smoke caught Hex's throat and he coughed.

Amber looked at him crossly. 'Don't think you'll get the sympathy vote.'

Alex looked at the two prostrate figures. In the firelight they looked peaceful. 'At least whatever they've been given has kept them quiet.'

Hex couldn't have spoken even if he hadn't been drugged. He needed to think. He'd nearly killed Amber. Maybe he wasn't cut out for this game any more.

32

AFTERMATH

Hex sat on a bench in the police station, waiting to give his statement. In front of him, the doors to the four interrogation rooms were closed, red lights indicating that interviews were in progress. The top officers of the Scottish Drug Enforcement Agency had been drafted in, and Amber, Alex, Paulo and Li were giving detailed statements.

The SDEA had been monitoring the situation ever since a routine check had picked up Paulo and Li's initial report to the local police about the game-keepers with the pills on the moor. Now Alpha Force were giving them virtually a complete picture of the operation – how the raw materials were stored in the lodge, transported to the factory on the moors inside deer carcasses; how the finished pills were transported to the bothy for packaging when there was an order; and how orders were shipped out from a lonely part of the coast by boat. The SDEA estimated the factory must be turning out several thousand pills a week, each batch with a street value of thousands of pounds.

Every spare policeman in the area was working on the case. They were removing evidence from the factory. They were going through the storeroom at the lodge. They had already dredged the cave, excavating tonnes of stone-filled barrels. Plus something else. They had found a decomposing body, shot in the throat at point-blank range.

Hex heard a creak as the swing door opened. A WPC showed out a man with a silvered beard. He was walking very slowly, as if he had had shocking news.

'How long do you need to keep him for?' he was asking the WPC.

'No more than a few days. We're trying to get the

coroner now. Once we've done the post-mortem and forensic examination we can release the body to you. You can start making funeral arrangements.'

The man nodded.

The WPC smiled sympathetically. 'It's not been a good holiday for you, has it, Mr Fletcher? The arson attack and now this.' She opened a door to show him through to reception.

Mr Fletcher. Martin Fletcher. Hex never forgot a name. Martin Fletcher was the hiker who had been trapped in the burning bothy with Alex and Paulo.

The two figures pushed out through the door into reception, leaving Hex alone with his thoughts again.

The light on one of the interrogation rooms went off and Alex came out. A plainclothes officer followed him with a clipboard. 'We'll be ready for you in five minutes,' he said to Hex.

Alex sat down beside Hex.

'You look pleased,' said Hex.

Alex was smiling. 'There's loads of evidence on the gamekeepers. The police think they were responsible for a factory in Glasgow a couple of years ago, but they shut up shop and scarpered.

That Ivanovich guy is a real coup. He's Russian Mafia and he's been wanted for ages. And then there's the body in the cave.'

'Who was he?' Hex grimaced. 'I'd like to know who I was sharing my bath with.'

'His name's James Fletcher. He's a professor of astronomy. He was staying at a bed and breakfast in March and he disappeared. They never found his body. Until now. They think he stumbled on something and was executed.'

'James Fletcher . . . Martin Fletcher . . . they must be brothers.' Hex saw Alex's bemused expression and explained. 'Martin Fletcher's the guy you were trapped in the bothy with, right? I just saw him here now. He was identifying someone.'

It made sense. 'Oh yes. He mentioned he had a brother who used to come here. Poor guy.' Alex shuddered. They had all nearly joined him.

Hex's mind was on the same thing. 'I suppose the two thugs who tried to kill me and Tiff have gone free, though.'

A smile of triumph played over Alex's lips. 'No they haven't. Remember Paulo spent all that time tinkering with the Range Rover? The tracker had been disconnected. He got it working again. The police picked them up about an hour down the road.'

Hex laughed quietly to himself. 'That is stylish,' he said. 'Very stylish.' He'd enjoy giving the evidence that ensured they stayed behind bars.

'When you were in the lodge,' said Alex, 'did you get any evidence on the laird?'

Hex thought. 'We overheard one conversation with the gamekeepers and the two heavies.'

'Was it taped?'

Hex shook his head.

Alex sighed. 'That's a pity. They've interviewed him but there's no actual evidence to pin on him. He says he's a city boy and lets his staff run the place. He had no idea that storeroom was full of the raw materials for drugs. Allegedly. They've looked into his history to see if he has a previous record but they can't even work out where he came from.'

'I'm sure he was the third man who came to the hostel,' said Hex. 'I remember his kilt. He was even wearing it later. But when I looked it up on the database, I saw it was a standard pattern to fob off tourists who want fake Scottish ancestry. Hardly enough to make a positive identification.'

Alex was grinning.

'What's the joke?'

'Just my puerile sense of humour. You looked up his kilt and you didn't find anything.'

Hex laughed and shoved him on the shoulder. 'Get out of here. I've got to go and give evidence in a minute. You'll upset my concentration.'

Alex stood up. 'I'm going to get some air. See you soon.' He pushed his way out through the swing doors.

Hex got out his palmtop. Now Alex had gone, he had a few minutes before the plainclothes officer came back to interview him. Just enough time . . .

There was a file he'd sent to a secure website while he was on the computer in the Glaickvullin shop.

Alex walked out into the car park. The sun was shining. It glinted off the windows of a taxi as it pulled in. It bleached out the ridges in the concrete drive. Behind, the moor rose up steeply, a cliff of purple heather.

A silver-haired figure came out of in the shadows of the building. He walked past Alex, his red Gore-Tex jacket over his arm. Martin Fletcher. Poor man, thought Alex. He looks lost. What's it like to find out your brother was murdered?

As he walked down the three concrete steps, he tripped. Alex rushed to help him up. He found his arm gripped in a fist of iron.

Martin Fletcher's grey eyes pierced his like two flints. He spoke in a low voice. 'I've had my eye on you. When you've finished here, come and see me at MI5.' He handed Alex a business card.

Alex looked at the card. It had a name and a number on it, nothing more.

The taxi pulled up. A petite figure got out and Alex caught a glimpse of pink shoes. Tiff, come to give evidence. She skipped up the steps and the taxi pulled away.

Martin Fletcher hadn't finished with Alex. 'Tell Hex when he wants a change of scene to e-mail johnsmith.'

'John Smith?' repeated Alex. But it wasn't quite the way Martin Fletcher had said it.

'johnsmith. All one word, lower case.'

He brushed the dust off his hands and walked away across the bleached car park.

Hex completed his task and put the palmtop back on standby. The plainclothes officer still hadn't come back. The outer door swung open again. Alex, thought Hex.

Instead of Alex's walking boots he saw faded pink Converse trainers.

It was Tiff. Her blonde hair was pushed up into a tweed cap and her face was pale. 'Mind if I sit here?'

It was the first time Tiff had asked for anything. Usually she demanded.

Hex moved over on the bench and she sat down. 'You OK?'

'I think I preferred the other pills I took.' She actually looked sheepish.

'Yeah,' said Hex. 'It looked like they were more fun.'

Tiff stared at her feet. 'I've been an idiot.'

This was a different Tiff talking. She was sad, like

the other evening when she'd taken the drug, but this time she knew what she was saying.

As she had then, she reminded Hex of so much. Particularly a spoilt rich girl who had been desperately unhappy. He had an urge to put his arm around her. Instead he grinned. 'You were more than an idiot.'

If he'd said that to the old Tiff, it would have lit the blue touch-paper. Instead she nodded and flexed her feet thoughtfully. 'I hated everything. I took it out on you guys. I was petty and spoiled, while there was all this life and death stuff going on around me. Tell everyone I'm sorry.'

Hex put his hand on her arm. 'A few years ago I hated everything too. Then I met some people.'

Tiff was quiet, thinking about what he'd said. 'Yeah,' she nodded. 'I know what you mean.' She turned to look at him. 'Keep in touch, right? Just as friends, nothing scary. Tell the others too.' She lifted her hand as if inviting him to arm-wrestle her. 'Respect.'

Hex clasped her hand. 'Respect.'

* * *

The sun was shining in Glasgow too, but the figure hunched over the computer had drawn the curtains across the window to block it out. Duncan Stewart was staring at the screen, unable to believe what he was seeing. But he had to. And it was serious. His bank account had been cleaned out.

Fists pummelling on the front door made him jump. No one hammered on doors like that – except the police.

The police were people Duncan Stewart liked to steer well clear of. The house was full of ecstasy pills; he'd just sold a shipment for London. Cautiously, he peered out of the window into the litter-strewn street below.

It wasn't the police. It was a guy with tattooed shoulders and a gold Rolex watch. Fergus. But why was he trying to hammer down the door? Were the police after him?

The thundering came again. 'Duncan!' he heard. 'Get up, ya lazy bastard.'

Duncan raced down the stairs. His heart was hammering. If the police were onto them, they'd better dump that ecstasy fast. He snatched open the door.

Fergus nearly ran over him as he came in. He slammed the door behind him. He looked furious.

Duncan asked first. 'Have you been busted?'

'My bank account's been cleaned out.'

Duncan felt a mixture of emotions. Relief, because he didn't have to get rid of all the drugs and scrub his house clean. But what Fergus said reminded him of what he'd just seen on his computer screen upstairs.

Fergus marched past him. 'Where's your hardware?' It was a rhetorical question; he seemed to know. He pulled open a cupboard and slid out a box of buckshot cartridges.

'My bank account's empty too. I just saw it this minute.'

'Yeah. Well I saw it twenty minutes ago. My son's done an audit trail. And guess whose fingerprints he found? That clever bastard Frank Allen.'

Fergus tossed Duncan a sawn-off shotgun and picked up another for himself.

'Laddie, I think it's time we went hunting in the north.'

33

THE BEACH

The police Land Rover pulled up by the shore of the Kyle. The driver, a young constable, turned round. 'Are you sure this is where you want to be dropped off?'

'Yes,' said Alex.

'I know the hostel's sealed off so you can't go back there, but we can find you a place in a B&B.'

'No,' said Alex. 'Here is fine.'

His four friends were already unloading gear from the boot. Sleeping rolls, waterproof plastic sheets, individual camping stoves and plenty of torches.

Hex helped Paulo put a rucksack over his good arm. The other arm was in a sling. He had been lucky. It was only a flesh wound. He had to take antibiotics and avoid activities that might split the wound open, but apart from that he was fine.

Li looked up at the sky. The clouds were high, the air still. 'Looks like we won't need those waterproofs.'

Amber looked up too. 'The forecast said it would be warm and dry.'

Alex picked up a rucksack. The constable was still looking bemused. Alex waved to him. He waved back, put the Land Rover in gear and drove away, shaking his head.

Alex led the way down the steep rocks onto the pebbly beach. The Kyle of Tongue was a still, silver triangle in front of him. Birds wheeled high in the sky, calling to each other. Otters and seals splashed in the water. The only other sound was the footsteps of his friends as they crunched along the beach behind him.

After a short walk Alex put his pack down. He'd found the perfect camping spot. A flat patch of rock that formed a low shelf, sheltered by a cliff.

Wordlessly, they followed his cue. They collected driftwood, finding plenty of pieces that had dried in the afternoon sunshine. They spread out sleeping bags, built a small hearth. Alpha Force could set up a camp virtually in their sleep. Many a long, hard day had ended with the same soothing routine.

Alex prepared his pièce de resistance. He dug a pit and got the fire going as the others combed the rocks for seafood. They brought back mussels, cockles, razor clams and scallops. Alex laid them on the hot stones and covered them with moss. A few minutes' cooking transformed them into a feast.

Alex pulled the scallop meat out of the shell and dropped it into his mouth. It was juicy, sweet, and quite delicious.

'You've been wanting to do this ever since we got to Scotland,' said Paulo.

Alex nodded, his eyes crinkled up with pleasure, his cheeks bulging. The pleasure on the others' faces was just as plain.

The sun was sinking into the horizon, lighting up the sky with red and purple. The Kyle was shimmering red. Somewhere on the opposite shore, about five kilometres away, was the cave where Alex and Amber had rescued Hex and Tiff. It would be sealed with police tape, but they were far enough away not to see it. It was there, but it merged with the dark shadows like a healed wound.

Paulo looked up into the vast sky. 'I can't believe I have to fly home tomorrow.'

Li tapped his sling with a razor-clam shell. 'You're going to be a lot of use on the ranch with that.'

Paulo gave her a grin. 'Yeah, but they're two pantaneiros down and it's calving season. All the freelances have got jobs. Half a cowboy is better than none.'

'Don't talk about going,' said Amber, licking her fingers. 'I've got to fly to Boston tomorrow and meet the board of my parents' company.'

Alex threw a razor-clam shell onto the discard pile. 'Do you think they'll be branching into adventure tourism?'

'If they do, I don't want to run it,' said Amber. 'It's too stressful. We can't even keep ourselves out of trouble.'

Paulo twitched his injured arm. 'Hey, do I get a refund?'

'No,' said Amber. 'You have to pay extra for a gunshot wound.'

'I know why he's really going back.' Li picked up a scallop. 'To show off his macho souvenir. He knows we won't be nearly as impressed as all the local girls.'

'You can come with me if you like,' said Paulo smoothly. 'Keep me under control.'

'Paulo,' said Alex, reaching for a mussel, 'you have my deepest sympathy. My dad got shot once and he said it's agony.'

'So, Li,' said Paulo, 'why are you standing me up tomorrow?'

'I was going to book a ticket to Shanghai. There's some family stuff I need to see to. But the police guy who interviewed me told me to call a recruiting officer he knows.'

'In drug enforcement?' said Alex. Another shell clinked onto the empties pile.

Li shook her head. 'No, it's something else. Nothing to do with drugs.' She wiped her hand on her trousers and took a card out of her pocket. It was plain with just a name and a number.

Hex hooted with laughter and produced a similar card. 'I got one too.'

Amber and Paulo both pulled cards out of their pockets. 'Snap.'

'I can do better than that,' said Alex. 'I've got two.'

'Pah,' said Amber. 'They probably gave one to Tiff as well.'

She was greeted with yowls of dismay, and had to duck as a barrage of empty shells whizzed towards her.

The meal was finished. Alex put more stones in the pit to raise the level of the fire and added more wood. Flames and smoke licked into the sky, flecked with wood particles.

The five friends swept away the shell debris and got into sleeping bags. The unpredictable Scottish weather had decided to be kind to them. The breeze off the sea was gentle and the night would be warm. The sky was now completely black, the stars clear and twinkling.

An airliner slid across the night sky as Amber lay back. Its wing lights winked red and white. 'I wish we didn't have to leave,' she said. The murmurs from the others told her they all felt the same.

Alex tucked his hands behind his head. 'Wouldn't it be great,' he said, 'if instead of having only our holidays together, we could end up working together?'

CHRIS RYAN'S TIPS FOR STANDARD OPERATING PROCEDURES

Like many of the world's elite forces, Alpha Force have standard operating procedures, or SOPs – a set of rules for carrying out missions to minimize the risk to personnel and ensure, as far as possible, that they are successful.

Two's company: Alpha Force don't go into an enemy area alone unless it's unavoidable. In the SAS we never worked alone, it was always in a minimum of pairs. Usually there were more than two of us in a squad, so we could keep people in reserve. That way, if someone's cover was blown we could swap them for someone else, or send in reinforcements if necessary. One of Alpha Force's strengths is that they have five members and they're quite distinctive. If the enemy has met a black American girl and a Chinese girl (Amber and Li), they won't necessarily connect them with two white English guys (Hex and Alex).

Keep in touch: Before any members of Alpha Force go into the field they arrange a time to call the others. A mission isn't just two people working on their own in the enemy territory – it's also the people back at base, who are making plans, deciding whether to send extra personnel and so on. If they don't call in when they're expected, the others at base know that something has gone wrong. So it's vital never to miss a situation report or 'sitrep', or the others might decide to send a rescue party.

Another reason the sitrep is essential is because the Alpha Force members back at base might have received new intelligence about the target. If they called the others the moment they received it, it might endanger them or blow the mission, so they wait until they know they can talk safely.

In the SAS we'd give a minimum of two sitreps every day to command control or base. Alpha Force, being a small squad, might not have a command control – all their members might be on active duty at one time. For instance, when Hex and Amber are in Glaickvullin Lodge and Alex, Paulo and Li are in the potholes, both groups are gathering and exchanging information and have to discuss their plans. In such a situation, they will agree beforehand to give a sitrep more frequently – say every couple of hours. Once they've agreed how frequently they will make sitreps, they will stick to it.

Sitreps aren't just for situations where you expect to encounter danger. Alex would never set out on one of his solo camping trips in Northumberland without letting someone know where he was going, and when he'd next be in touch. When Paulo goes for a ride on his parents' ranch, he leaves a message saying where he's gone and how long he expects to be. If you're going somewhere alone, such as camping, you should do the same.

Use passwords: If Alpha Force have to rendezvous with someone who they haven't met before, they have to make sure they can identify them positively. If they don't, they might draw an innocent bystander into their mission by mistake, or they might even be duped into taking an enemy agent into their confidence. They will take a physical description of the agent they're meeting, but they won't rely on that alone because it's not that easy to recognize someone just from a description like 'dark hair, medium build and glasses'. They will use a password.

A password has to be more than just one word, because that's too conspicuous. For instance, if your password was 'elephant', you might walk up to several people with dark hair, medium build and glasses and see if they said 'elephant' to you, but most of them will be ordinary members of the public and you might get some very odd looks! Also, if enemy agents were watching they would soon spot what you were up to. Instead, Alpha Force prearrange to have a short conversation with the person they are meeting. For instance, when they spot someone with dark hair, medium build and glasses, they will ask them, 'Has a man with a black dog walked past?' An innocent stranger – or an enemy agent – might say no – or yes if it was in a common dog-walking spot. But the real agent will have agreed to say something more distinctive, such as 'No, it was a Dalmatian.' It's very unlikely that anyone would give such a complicated answer by chance.

Keep your cover: If Alpha Force have to create fake identities, they practise using them before they go into the field. If Amber has to go undercover as, say, Roz, she practises introducing herself as Roz. As she's using a different name from usual, it would be very easy to look embarrassed or hesitate, which an enemy might spot. Amber would also have to get used to listening out for people trying to attract her attention by calling 'Roz' – it looks very odd if you don't respond when someone calls your name! It works the other way too – if she wasn't prepared, someone could easily blow her cover by shouting 'Hi, Amber!'

A fake identity is more than just a name. Amber also has to work out what town Roz comes from, what school she went to. These are the kinds of question strangers might ask casually – or enemies might ask if they wanted to check you out. Amber has to pick a home town for Roz – and be able to answer questions about it. An enemy might, for instance, ask her if the store at the crossroads still sells marzipan doughnuts. It might be a trick question because there may be no shop there at all; it may be a school!

Another thing Alpha Force bear in mind when constructing a fake identity is what their own appearance and accents say about them. Hex has a London accent and it might be hard to believe he came from Scotland – or the USA!

Get information: If Alpha Force are infiltrating an enemy area, they will get as much information about it as they can. Hex spends a lot of time collecting information from his sources on the Internet. If possible they will also talk to people who have been into the area, and look at satellite pictures. There's no substitute for intelligence.

Rehearse: In the caves, Alex, Paulo and Li make a diagram while they are working out their plan to smoke out the gamekeepers. That cave was quite a simple site, with few entrances and exits, but many targets will not be so straightforward. If they were infiltrating an enemy camp, there might be many possible angles of approach, dead spots, places to hide, routes in and routes out. The diagram makes sure everyone has the same mental picture of how they will get in, where they are going and so on. Another vital point is that when they've finished with the diagram and are about to move on, they are careful to destroy it. They never know who might stumble on it.

Alpha Force also spend time practising the final phase of the smoke-out operation so that they can execute it swiftly and efficiently. In the SAS, if we had time, we would try to find a similar camp to the one we were infiltrating and rehearse for real. We'd practise absolutely everything – not just getting in and out, but our order of approach, laying-up points (LUPs), where to dump equipment, who would cut the fence. An operation must be slick to keep the element of surprise – you don't want to waste precious seconds trying to remember who's got the wire cutters and getting them out from the bottom of their bergen!

If Alpha Force have to use unfamiliar equipment, they rehearse with that too. They might have just thirty seconds to set up a camera, make sure it's working and well concealed. It's hopeless if they start fumbling, drop it, can't find the on button.

Alpha Force have often had to change their clothes in enemy territory to blend in – and even this takes practice. Try it yourself – get a mate to time you while you put on a disguise (make sure they don't peek!). Can you get all the buttons done up, everything the right way round and look neat and shipshape in 60 seconds? To make it even more challenging, try the same thing in a darkened cupboard!

Assess risk: Although Alpha Force frequently end up in danger, they always plan not to! Before they go into an enemy area they make sure their plan allows them to stay hidden and get out safely. They never just take this for granted – if they don't have a proper entry and escape, they don't go in. Otherwise, if they are captured, not only might they be hurt or interrogated, they might endanger an entire mission – which could be of national importance.

Man down!: If someone does get injured, the operation's over. The number one priority is to get them out and to help. Once the injured person is in a safe place, though, it might be possible to go back in with a change of personnel. For instance, if Paulo sprained his ankle and had to be extricated, he might be taken out to where Li was guarding the spare kit at an LUP, then Li could go in in his place while he guards the bergens. This also means that whoever's left on back-up duty has to be prepared for a more active role at a moment's notice – it would be no good if Li was having a snooze or was engrossed in a book when the others needed reinforcements.

Never underestimate the enemy: No matter how simple a task may be, Alpha Force assume the enemy will be as tough, alert and well trained as they are. They are never slipshod about planning and preparation. And they stay in training, practising their skills so they don't get rusty. Many times their lives have depended on how fast they can run or how strong they are – so all of them put in regular hours in the gym and many miles running, cycling and swimming. They never know when they might need it.

BE SAFE!

Chris Ryan

Random House Children's Books and Chris Ryan would like to make it clear that this advice is given for use in a serious situation only, where your life could be at risk. We cannot accept any liability for inappropriate usage in normal conditions.

Have you read all the Alpha Force books? Here's a chance to test your survival skills with the ALPHA FORCE QUIZ!

1. **What should you do if someone gets a snakebite?**
a) Keep the victim calm, suck out the venom and try to get medical help quickly
b) Keep the victim calm, cut out the venom and try to get medical help quickly
c) Keep the victim calm, wash out the venom and try to get medical help quickly

2. **Which African animal kills more humans than any other?**
a) Hippopotamus
b) Crocodile
c) Lion

3. **What are the common symptoms of shock?**
a) Hot, clammy skin, and a slow pulse and lack of movement
b) Cold, sweaty skin, a feeble but rapid pulse and shakiness
c) The victim won't show any noticeable signs

4. **What chemical creates an antiseptic when added to water?** (Hint: Alex carries it in his survival kit in *Desert Pursuit*)
a) Potassium permanganate
b) Sodium Chloride
c) Sulphur

5. **Roughly how long can you survive without water?**
a) One day
b) Three days
c) Five days

6. **How long can the average human survive without food?**
a) One week
b) Two weeks
c) Three weeks

7. **If you sprain an ankle but have to keep moving, you should**
a) Keep your boot on
b) Take your boot off and strap up the ankle
c) Take your boot off and leave the ankle unsupported

8. **What's the internationally recognised format to use with any signal when you need help?**
a) Repeat any signal three times
b) Repeat any signal four times
c) Repeat any signal five times

9. **If you're stuck without supplies, what is the best thing for washing out wounds?**
a) Saliva
b) Urine
c) Tears

10. **What are the symptoms of salt deprivation?**
a) Sweating and feeling nauseous
b) Feeling dizzy and tired
c) All of the above

11. **What should you *not* do if a leech attaches itself to your skin?**

a) Use heat to try and make it drop off

b) Pull it off

c) Use petrol or alcohol to try and make it drop off

12. **What should you do if you find yourself confronting a big cat?**

a) Run

b) Shout and wave your arms

c) Curl up into a ball

13. **What's the best thing to store your survival kit in?**

a) A plastic bag

b) A waterproof box or tin

c) A cloth bag

14. **Which of these should you never drink?**

a) Sea water

b) Freshwater that hasn't been boiled or sterilized

c) Both of the above

15. **Which of the options below would be the best place to build a shelter?**

a) Bottom of a valley

b) Hilltop

c) On the edge of a forest

16. **What's the Morse code signal for SOS?**

a) dot, dot, dot/dash, dash, dash/dot, dot, dot

b) dot, dot, dash/dot, dot, dash/dot, dot, dash

c) dash, dash, dash/dot, dot, dot/dash, dash, dash

17. What can you rub underneath your eyes to reduce the glare from snow and help prevent snow blindness?

a) Leaf sap
b) Charcoal
c) Chalk

18. Which of these symptoms means you might be getting frostbite?

a) Prickly sensation in hands or feet and numb, waxy-looking patches
b) Burning sensation in hands or feet and red, scaly patches
c) No sensation in hands or feet and red, scaly patches

19. If your body temperature drops faster than your body can generate heat, what are you suffering from?

a) Hyperthermia
b) Dehydration
c) Hypothermia

20. What colour flare should you use for an SOS signal?

a) Blue
b) Green
c) Red

Have you got what it takes to be a member of Alpha Force?
Turn over to find out the answers and see how good your
survival skills are!

Chris Ryan

ANSWERS

1.   c. If you suck out the venom you may poison yourself and attempting to cut out the venom may drive it further into the bloodstream.

2.   a. Hippos are very aggressive and territorial and they can run 100 metres in 9 seconds!

3.   b

4.   a

5.   b. You can survive for longer without food but not without water!

6.   c

7.   a. Otherwise your ankle will swell and you won't be able to put your boot on again.

8.   a

9.   b

10.   c

11.   b. If you pull the leech off the head will remain under your skin and could cause a poisonous reaction.

12.   b. Making yourself look as big and threatening as possible is the only way to deter a large cat. Running will trigger its kill response!

13.   b

14.   c

15.   c. On the edge of a forest is a good option as you will be able to see anything that approaches. A valley could be damp and a hilltop could be exposed to wind.

16.   a

17.   b

18.   a

19.   c

20.   c